BLACK Hatted COWBOYS

BRYAN MARLOWE

T0315965

BLACK Hatted COWBOYS

MEMOIRS
Cirencester

Published by Memoirs

MEMOIRS
PUBLISHING

25 Market Place, Cirencester, Gloucestershire, GL7 2NX
info@memoirsbooks.co.uk www.memoirspublishing.com

ISBN:978-1-909304-68-0

Let us cast out the works of darkness and put on the armour of light.

Romans Chap 13, v. 14 (paraphrased)

FOR KATHLEEN - MY INSPIRATION

CHAPTER ONE

Laurence Howard, who lived alone in a two-bedroom second floor flat in Blackheath Village, south-east London, was sitting at his kitchen table eating his evening meal of sardines on toast, washed down with a mug of strong sweet tea. Suddenly, the buzz of the doorbell disturbed his reading of the evening paper. 'Who can that be calling on me at this hour?' he mused. He drained his mug, rose reluctantly, and went to the front door. He opened the door to see a tall, rotund and red-faced police sergeant and a young, blonde female constable standing in the doorway.

Howard looked at them questioningly.

The sergeant cleared his throat noisily before he spoke. 'Are you Laurence Howard?'

'Yes, I am. What do you want?'

'May we come in, Mr Howard? We have something to tell you that may be better said inside.'

'Yes, of course, come in.' Howard stood aside to let them in.

He led them into his sparsely furnished, but neatly arranged, sitting room.

The police officers stood in the middle of the room, waiting to be invited to sit down.

'Please take a seat and tell me why you're here,' Howard said.

The two police officers sat on the two-seater chesterfield while Howard occupied the only other seat in the room—a high-backed leather Chesterfield chair.

The sergeant cleared his throat. 'I'm very sorry to have to be the bearer of some very bad news for you, sir.' He spoke in a voice that was well-practised at breaking bad news. 'I regret to have to tell you that your mother and father were killed late last night and that your sister was seriously injured and is now in Lewisham hospital. It was she who told us where you lived.'

Howard was stunned by the news. After a moment's silence he recovered and said in a strained voice, 'How and where were they killed?'

'There was an explosion in their house and they were both killed instantaneously by the blast. Your sister suffered severe bruising to her body and her left shoulder blade and arm were fractured by falling debris.'

'What caused the explosion?'

'The matter is being investigated, but it is thought to have been caused by a gas leak.'

'A gas leak?' Then Howard remembered—his father had said he was arranging for a new gas boiler to be installed. Howard, being a clerk of works employed by the Greenwich Borough Council, had told his father to leave it to him to arrange for a Corgi trained gas fitter to carry out the work. But with the sudden onset of below freezing temperatures his father must have decided they urgently needed a replacement boiler and gone ahead and found someone, probably unqualified, to fit one

The sergeant said: 'Would you like PC Roberts to make you a hot drink, sir?'

'No thank you. Just tell me where my parents are now.'

The sergeant sighed deeply. 'They've been taken to the hospital mortuary. You'll be notified when a coroner's court is to be convened. After that has been held the bodies of your parents will be released for their funeral to take place.'

As much as Howard was upset by the news of the death of his parents, being a long serving soldier who had served in battle zones and witnessed the deaths of close friends and comrades in arms, he was able to remain stoic and seemingly unmoved when faced with sudden death.

The two police officers were beginning to feel uncomfortable. Both had visited the homes of the families who had lost close relatives, but had never before witnessed such stoicism as was being displayed by Howard.

The sergeant said: 'Well, sir, if there's nothing we can do, we'll be on our way.'

'No, there's nothing anyone can do for me. I'll be going to the hospital to see my sister, as soon as you've gone.'

Howard led them to the door. As they passed into the hall the sergeant turned and said: 'Please accept our sincere condolences for your loss, and if there is anything you might need help with, our Families' Liaison Officer will call in to see you.'

'Thanks for the offer Sergeant, but I think I can cope with what I have to do. Goodnight.'

'Goodnight.' the officers replied in unison.

Howard watched them as they walked down the corridor to the top of the stairs and then closed the door. Returning to the kitchen, he cleared his supper things. His army service had trained him to "clear as you go."

* * * * *

Not being confident of finding somewhere to park at, or near the hospital, Howard phoned for a taxi. Arriving at the hospital, he went to the main reception desk and spoke to the first receptionist that became free. "Good evening. My name is Larry Howard and I've been told that my sister, Louise Howard. is a patient here. Could you please tell me the ward she is in?'

The receptionist nodded and logged into her desktop computer. After a few seconds of tapping keys she said: 'She's in Florence Ward—it's on the third floor. Just report to the ward sister and she'll be able to give you information about your sister's condition.'

Howard thanked her and climbed the stairs to the third floor. He resisted the temptation to go straight into the ward to see Louise and went to the ward sister's station.

'Good evening, Sister. My name is Howard and I've

come to see my sister, Louise Howard. How is she?'

'She was severely injured last night, in what I understand from the paramedics was an explosion in her home. She underwent surgery shortly after she was admitted. She was in a lot of pain, but has been given analgesics and her condition is now stable. If she's asleep, please don't waken her. She needs all the rest she can get.'

'Thank you, Sister, I promise not to disturb her. But tell me, does she know that our parents were killed in the explosion?'

'Yes, I'm afraid so. The police came to speak to her this afternoon. They wanted to know if she had a next of kin, or someone who might help them find someone to notify."

'Yes, they called on me this evening. That's why I'm here.'

Howard entered the ward and went to Louise's bedside. He looked down at her, seeing her bandaged head and plaster-encased arm and shoulder. Her eyes were closed, but as soon as he sat on the bedside chair, her eyes opened and a glint of recognition showed in them at the sight of him.

Howard smiled, leant forward and whispered, 'If you'd rather not speak, I'll understand.'

Louise turned to face him and stretched out her good arm. Howard took hold of her hand.

'Larry, it's so terrible… Mum and Dad killed… I just can't believe it.'

'Try not to think about what happened. Just rest and get better. I'll come in to see you every evening and I'll get my spare bedroom prepared for you to occupy as soon as you're fit enough to be discharged. Is there anything I can bring in for you?'

'I don't suppose any of my personal belongings and clothes survived the fire.'

'No, I suppose not, but don't worry about things like that. As soon as they let you out I'll take you shopping for a new wardrobe. The insurance company can pay for that, and don't worry about your school. I'll let your head-teacher know what's happened.'

'Oh, Larry, I'm so lucky to have a big brother who can take care of things.'

'Okay, that's enough. Now get back to sleep and I'll be in to see you tomorrow.'

Louise gave his hand a gentle squeeze and he bent over and kissed her forehead.

Before leaving the ward, he gave the ward clerk his telephone number and said, 'If my sister, Louise Howard, wants anything brought in please telephone this number before seven in the morning or after five-thirty in the evening. Thank you and goodnight.'

CHAPTER TWO

As soon as Howard got into work the following morning, he went straight to his line manager's office. 'I'm going to need a few days off from today, Geoff.'

'That's a bit short notice, Larry. Is it for something special?'

'*Something special!* Two *days ago my parents were killed and my sister was severely injured and has been admitted to hospital!* So I've quite a lot of things to take care of.'

Geoff's face reddened. 'I'm sorry to hear that, Larry. Of course, you can take whatever time you need. How did it happen?'

'There was an explosion in their house. They were killed instantly and my sister was seriously injured.'

'How awful for you! Is there anything we can do to help you in any way?'

'Not really. My sister will be moving in with me when she gets out of hospital and I want to help get her settled in. Then there's the funeral to arrange, letters to be sent to their pension authorities and insurance claims. Everything in the house was destroyed or damaged.'

'Has it been ascertained as to what caused the explosion, Larry?'

'It's being investigated, but it's most likely to have been caused by a gas leak from a recently installed boiler.'

'Good God, not another incident of an inefficiently installed gas boiler! It sounds like your father must have unwittingly hired a *cowboy* to carry out the work.'

'Yes, it looks very much like that. In a way I feel responsible.'

Geoff's eyebrows rose. 'How do you make that out?'

'Well, I did promise to arrange for a qualified fitter to do the job. But I suppose, with the bad weather we've been having recently, he decided he couldn't wait for me to recommend someone and decided to go ahead and get the job done.'

'Have you any idea who he employed?'

'No, but I intend to find out—people like that ought to be put away.'

'You're certainly right there, Larry. If the person responsible is found he ought to be charged with manslaughter.'

'Well, I'll not waste any more of your time, Geoff. I'll go and have a word with the police to see if they've found out anything more. I'll get back to work as soon as I've done what I've got to do.'

'Before you go, Larry, I'd like you to know that I'm very sorry about what's happened. I knew your mother and father. You couldn't meet a nicer couple. Let me know when the funeral is to be held. I'd like to attend. And give my very best wishes to your sister for her speedy recovery.'

'Thanks, Geoff, and cheerio for now.'

'Cheerio, Larry. I do hope everything works out for you and Louise.'

* * * * *

Howard approached the enquiry office in the central police station. An unoccupied constable came to the counter. 'How can we help you, sir?'

'Good morning Constable. My name is Laurence Howard. My father and mother were killed in an explosion in their home two days ago. I'd like to speak to whoever is dealing with the case.'

'It'll be with the CID. I'll see if the officer concerned is available.'

The constable went to the back of the office, picked up a telephone and tapped three numbers. When he got a response, he spoke for about a minute before putting down the phone and returning to the counter. 'DS Parsons is the officer dealing with this matter. He said he'd pop down and have a word with you. Would you go and sit in the waiting area?' The constable pointed across the entrance hall.

Howard joined the other members of the waiting public. Some looked villainous enough to be in the cells. He thought they were probably snouts (informers) who'd cross the line between larceny and the law for a monetary reward.

DS Parsons, short, overweight and unshaven, dressed in faded blue jeans, a loud check shirt and a black leather jacket, appeared a few minutes later and walked straight up to Howard. 'Are you Mr Howard?' he asked in a low voice that he didn't want heard by the other waiting public.

'Yes, Sergeant,' Howard nodded.

'Come with me,' he replied and led Howard into a room with a door bearing the sign "Interview Room 3." The only items in the room were a table, three chairs and a waste paper basket. There was no recording equipment in the room and it was not soundproofed. Howard guessed it was probably reserved for interviewing members of the public who were not under arrest or suspected of being involved in crime.

Parsons sat down and Howard sat down on the other side of the table.

Parsons produced a notebook and a biro from his jacket pocket.

Before Parsons could say anything, Howard said, 'It seems to me we may be at cross-purposes, Sergeant. I came here to enquire if anything had been found out about the death of my parents and yet you seem to be preparing to question me!'

'Just routine, we need to keep a record of any inquiries we make or statements we take. So, what's your full name and address, sir?'

'Laurence Ralph Howard, Flat 5, 28 Blackheath Lane, SE3 8PZ.'

'What's your date of birth?'

'31st January, 1969.'

'And what is your occupation?'

'I'm a clerk of works employed by the Greenwich Borough Council. And, if it is required for your records, I'm five feet eleven inches or, if you are metrically minded, 1.78 metres tall and my inside leg measurement is 31 inches, or 81 centimetres!'

'Oh, so you're a wise-guy, eh,' Parsons said, banging his right fist on the table.

'Not particularly, but I can't see why you require all this information. It seems like unnecessary bureaucracy to me! What I want and need to know from you is how my parents were killed! It has been suggested to me that it was the result of a gas explosion. Are you able to confirm this was the cause and the name of the contractor who fitted the boiler?'

'Yes, it was a gas leak that caused the explosion, but nobody seems to know who installed the boiler. We're still looking for him and when we do find him he's likely to face prosecution.'

'I should certainly hope so. Tell me, have enquiries been made with my parents' neighbours?'

'Yes, an elderly woman who lives across the road from your parents' house said that she saw a white van parked outside the house a few days ago and a middle-aged man and a youth carrying boxes into the house.'

'So, that's it then—no name on the van, no registered number and no description of the two men?'

'No, the old girl was a bit past it and we couldn't get anything more from her than we did. As soon as we make an arrest we'll let you know. I'm sure you'll want to attend the trial.'

'I hope I don't have to wait too long for your call, Sergeant.'

'No, be assured, Larry, we'll give the investigation top priority,' Parsons replied with a humourless laugh.

Howard made no reply as he left the room. If the *cowboy* gas fitter was to be found it looked as though it might be down to him to find him, and find him he was determined to do.

CHAPTER THREE

Gary Bottrell, was a 35-year-old, ex-corporal in the Royal Military Police, who had been court martialled, stripped of his rank, awarded 56-days detention and dishonourably discharged from the Army for causing grievous bodily harm to a prisoner in his charge. Since his discharge, five years ago, he had lived alone in a one-bedroom flat in Deptford. He was employed as a door manager in a seedy gambling club in New Cross.

Two months previously his wife, Tracey, from whom he had been separated since his discharge, and his 11-year-old daughter, Wendy, were found dead in their beds, having been poisoned by carbon monoxide gas. The gas leak had been traced to a faulty connection in the flue pipe from a newly installed boiler. Because no safety alarm had been fitted and the gas being odourless, the victims had not been alerted to the escape of the poisonous fumes.

The police investigating the deaths had learned from Mrs Bottrell's next-door neighbours, the name of the man who had installed the replacement boiler. He had been arrested and charged with manslaughter by criminal neglect and was bailed to appear in court in two months' time.

Bottrell was not much sorrowed by the death of his wife. In his mind she'd been an utter bitch and had left him after he had been court-martialled. Anyway, her dying saved him the trouble and expense of divorcing her. But Wendy was another matter—he had idolised her and he had made a secret vow to take revenge on Steve Capstick who had, through his criminal negligence, been responsible for her death.

How he could achieve his intention was on his mind as he sat watching the evening news on his television, while eating a pizza, delivered earlier that evening. Bottrell didn't do cooking and since he had been living on his own had always ordered takeaway meals from the various convenience food outlets in the local area.

An item of local news drew his immediate attention. It reported the deaths of an elderly retired couple who were killed when an explosion, believed to have been caused by a gas leak, had destroyed their home. Their daughter was seriously injured in the blast. A BBC reporter had interviewed the victims' son, who was a clerk of works employed by the local authority. He told the reporter that he was convinced that faulty workmanship was the cause of the leak and laid the blame against a "cowboy builder". He went on to say the police were investigating the incident and hoped that anyone who had any knowledge of who might have been employed to carry out the work at his parents' home would pass the information to the local police.

Bottrell was interested enough in what he'd heard to

leave his unfinished pizza. If this man, what was his name...Oh yes...Howard... had revenge in his mind, calling on him to tell him of his own family tragedy might be worthwhile. They could share their grief. Perhaps even develop a comradeship. 'Yes, I'll call on him and take him out for a drink,' he decided. There was no knowing where such an arrangement might lead them, and it would be no problem getting his full address from the Voters' List.

* * * * *

Bottrell's hours of work were from six in the evening until two the following morning. His days off were Sunday and Monday.

On the following Monday morning, he went to the Council Offices and checked the Electoral Roll. It took him only three minutes to locate and make a note of Laurence Howard's address.

At eight o'clock, by which time he thought Howard would have been home for a couple of hours and had time to have had his evening meal, he drove to Howard's address and parked in a neighbouring street. It occurred to him that it might be wiser not to be seen visiting Howard. He pressed the doorbell and within a few seconds a man answered the door.

'Good evening, sir, I hope I've not disturbed you,' Bottrell said in an obsequious tone. 'I'm looking for a Mr Laurence Howard.'

Howard half smiled. 'Well, you've found Mr Laurence

Howard, but I'll not decide whether or not you've disturbed me until you tell me why you're calling on me.'

'Well, sir, it's rather a delicate matter. It concerns the dreadful accident that happened to your family.'

Howard looked steadily at Bottrell for several seconds, noting his smart, well-groomed appearance; his initial appraisal suggested that the man was some sort of door-to-door salesman.

Bottrell, realizing that his overly long and untidy hairstyle might be off-putting for more traditionally minded members of the public, such as a clerk of works for a local authority, had had a haircut that morning. He wanted to be taken seriously.

'Who are you?'

'My name is Gary Bottrell, Mr Howard, and I'm not selling anything.'

'Well, you better come in and tell me what this is all about.' Howard stood aside to allow him to enter. He led him into the sitting room and motioned to him to sit down on the chesterfield.

'So, what brings you to my door, Mr Bottrell?'

'I saw on the television news that your parents had been killed in an explosion and that your sister had been injured.'

Howard looked questioningly at Bottrell. 'Well, that doesn't explain why you have called on me.'

'No, I'm sorry—perhaps I should explain. A few weeks ago my own family was killed in a similar accident. There wasn't an explosion but my wife and my daughter were poisoned by carbon monoxide gas, while they slept.'

'Then I suppose we should be offering each other our sincere condolences. But I don't see what is similar about their deaths.'

'Well, I've given a lot of thought to this and I'm firmly convinced that both accidents occurred because of the faulty workmanship of incompetent tradesmen in the building trades and known as "cowboy builders"!'

'Yes, in the case of my parents' death, I'm inclined to agree, but neither I nor the police have any knowledge of who was responsible for the faulty work.'

'Would I be right in thinking that you want the police to find out who was responsible and charge him for what might be considered manslaughter?'

'Of course, I would. And, if he was found guilty, I'd like to see him put away for a very long time!'

'I know who was responsible for the death of my wife and daughter. He's been arrested and charged with manslaughter. He's out on bail until his case comes up in about a month. Mind you, I have to admit that if I could get my hands around his throat I'd choke the life out of the bastard!'

'Hmm… I can understand the strength of your feelings, but if you did that you'd be facing a charge of at least manslaughter yourself. Best let the law deal with this. Being how there are so many of these cases cropping up, feeling against such people is very strong now.'

'Public feeling against *cowboy builders* might be very strong, but I've researched the matter and found that those who have been responsible for the death of their clients have not been sentenced to more than four years. And they probably serve no more than two!'

'Now, Gary, I can see you're understandably very upset by what has happened. I too am much saddened and angry by the death of my parents, but having been a long-time soldier I'm probably more stoical in dealing with the death of family and friends.'

'You, an ex-army man, Larry, if we're on first names. What regiment were you in?'

'I was a WO2 in the REME. I did pensionable service.'

'Oh, so I'd have had to call you "sir". I was just a corporal Redcap. I came out early to spend more time with my family,' Bottrell lied.

'Can I offer you a drink, Gary?'

'Yes, *sir*,' Bottrell replied with a wide grin. 'But I have to be honest and tell you that I'm a lager and whisky drinker.'

'Oh, that's a pity, because I don't drink beer and I've no whisky to hand. I only drink wine based drinks.'

'Well, I'll tell you what—let's go out to a local pub. I feel much better about everything after our little talk and if you've nothing better to do I'd like our discussion to continue.'

'Why not—there's not much worth watching on television tonight,' Howard said with a smile. 'Hang on for a minute while I get a jacket.'

Outside, Bottrell took the lead. 'The place I have in

mind is *The Duke of York* and it's not far from here so we won't need to use a car. Anyway, a couple of stiff whiskies and I'd be well over the limit.'

They arrived at *The Duke of York* about ten minutes later. 'This is the place I had in mind,' said Bottrell, pushing the door open.

'It's a new one on me,' replied Howard, following Bottrell to a corner in the dimly lit bar. There were only three other men in the bar who sat in the opposite corner talking in low voices.

'I'll get these,' said Bottrell. 'What's yours, Larry?'

'A glass of the house's best red wine will be fine for me.'

Bottrell went to the bar and ordered the drinks. He returned with a large glass of wine and a double whisky.

They lifted their glasses and said: 'Cheers!'

They sat drinking silently for a few minutes, both at a loss to know what to talk about. Bottrell broke the silence.

'When you said that you'd like to find out who had fitted your parents' new boiler, it occurred to me that one way to do that would be to go into your father's favourite pub and have a couple of drinks at the bar and chat up the bar person. Get onto the subject of house repairs and say that you need a new boiler fitting. Say that you'd pay cash up front to avoid paying VAT. Then ask the bar person if they know of anyone who might do the job. Of course, if you know the first name of the bloke who fitted your father's boiler it would be easy. Blokes in that type of business rarely divulge their surnames. You could just ask if Tom, Dick, Harry, or whatever he's called, had been in recently.'

'You seem to be taking a lot for granted. What makes

you think my father dealt with tradesmen he met in a pub?'

'Why not—where else would he go—the Citizens' Advice Bureau? He must have been in his late sixties and he'd surely use a local pub. He did drink, didn't he?'

'He was 76 and he'd used the same pub for years. And, by the way, I had told him that I would recommend a Corgi qualified fitter to do the job. But he became impatient and went ahead and took on a chap, who turned out to be a cowboy fitter.'

'Well it's worth a try then, isn't it? If you wait for the police to come up with something, you could be waiting a long time.'

'I'll give it some thought. Now let's change the subject. You appear to be in need of replenishment,' added Howard, looking at Bottrell's empty glass.

'Yes, is it the same again for you?'

'Yes, but I'm in the chair this time,' Howard replied, picking up the empty glasses and taking them to the bar. Returning with the drinks, he set them down and said, 'So where did your time in the army take you, Lew?'

'Oh… er… mostly in the UK—I did tours of duty in Northern Ireland, Catterick Garrison, and I spent some time on the staff of the detention barracks in Colchester.' Bottrell had never been a member of the staff of the detention barracks—he had been there undergoing a term of detention following a court martial for causing actual bodily harm to a prisoner in his charge.

'So you didn't serve in Iraq or Afghanistan?'

'No, I suppose I was lucky to miss those campaigns.

We lost quite a few Redcaps there.'

'Yes, that was a pretty grim incident when half a dozen of your regiment were massacred.'

'I suppose you, being in the REME, had a pretty cushy time behind the lines when you were on active service.'

Howard's eyebrows rose. 'Don't you believe it, old chap. I was once attached to No.11 Explosive Ordnance Disposal Regiment and our job was defusing those deadly improvised explosive devices that were scattered around the Helmand Province, claiming the lives of many members of the coalition forces.'

'Hmm... so I expect you were glad to retire when you did.'

'On the contrary, I didn't want to retire so early. I was in the frame for a commission, but while I was in the army I hadn't spent much time with my family and thought if I stayed in until I was about fifty-five, I'd have very little time with them and, not only that, I would probably have had difficulty in finding suitable employment. Speaking of which, what do you do to earn your daily bread?'

Bottrell pondered for a few seconds before he answered. 'Oh, I manage a sports club. It doesn't pay much but I see it as a worthwhile occupation, which provides a useful service, for the sports-minded. '

'Yes, I'm sure it does,' said Howard with a broad smile, thinking, 'One thing for certain, this guy's a bit of a bull-shitter.'

'But, Larry, getting back to cowboy builders and the misery and sometimes death they cause their victims, don't you feel like taking revenge on the man who was responsible for the death of your parents?'

Howard stroked his chin, deep in thought before he answered. 'Yes, of course I do. I expect if I got hold of the man, I'd give him a good thrashing before I turned him over to the police.'

Bottrell grimaced. 'A good thrashing, eh?—I'd like to see the bastards hanged!'

Howard shook his head. 'Yes, they might deserve that sort of fate, but in this country they don't even hang people for premeditated murder anymore.'

'More's the pity!' Bottrell snapped.

Howard was beginning to tire of Bottrell's company. He drained his glass—Bottrell had long since finished his drink—and said, 'I think I'll call it a night, Gary, I've got a lot to do before my sister is discharged from hospital and moves in with me.'

'Okay, Larry, but remember what I said and keep in touch.'

They walked back with hardly a word spoken to where Bottrell had parked his car and Howard watched him drive away, and then returned to his flat, thinking that he was not sorry that it was probably the last he would see of Bottrell.

CHAPTER FOUR

During the two days before Louise was discharged from hospital, Howard spent the time redecorating his spare room and buying new curtains and oddments of furniture more fitting for a woman's bedroom.

On the day of her discharge from the hospital, he went to collect her in his car. Her left shoulder was strapped up and her left arm was in a plaster cast, but she was no longer in pain and was overjoyed to be met by her brother and looking forward to settling in the room he had prepared for her. She had very little baggage; nothing had survived the explosion and fire in her parents' home. The only clothes she had were those Howard had bought for her to travel from the hospital.

As soon as they arrived at the flat Larry quickly prepared a tuna salad lunch. They sat with cups of coffee after lunch and talked about the arrangements that needed to be made for their parents' funeral.

'Don't worry about anything, Louise: I'll take care of everything. There is just one thing you need to do though and that is to make a list of all your clothes and personal effects damaged or destroyed in the fire. Let me have it as soon as you can and then I'll submit an insurance claim.'

'Right, I'll get on to that as soon as I can. What about the house insurance, though? I feel sure that dad held an insurance policy for the house, but I suppose it was destroyed in the fire. The house was absolutely gutted— I was lucky to have escaped with my life.'

'Yes, you certainly were! Don't worry about the policy document, I know the company dad was insured with and I'll get on to them to send me a claim form. When I tell them what happened they'll send someone to view the ruin that was once our home. By the way, did dad mention to you the name of the company that fitted the replacement boiler?'

Louise's forehead creased in thought. 'No, when I asked him he just said that Steve and his lad had done a quick and reasonably priced job in replacing the boiler for cash.'

'Hmm… so the man who did the job was called Steve? That's a useful piece of information to follow up. Do you happen to know the name of the pub that dad was using?'

'Yes, it was *The Star and Garter* on Blake Street. What are you going to do—report this to the police?'

'Yes, something like that. But never mind all that now. Our first priority is to take you shopping for a new wardrobe. Do you feel up to it this afternoon?'

Louise's face lit up. 'I can't think of anything I'd rather do. I feel well enough to go shopping and anyway, it'll be easy because I can get all I need at Marks and Spencer.'

'That's great! You just put your legs up and have a rest for an hour and then we'll be off.'

They returned to the flat four hours later, laden with

clothing and toiletries. They had eaten in a restaurant a few door from the department store, so Larry spent the evening putting everything away in Louise's room.

'Thank you, Larry; you've done a wonderful job of stowing everything away in such an orderly manner. I could never have made such a good use of the space available.'

'You can thank my army training for that,' Larry replied with a broad grin. 'Now I think you ought to get an early night. I've connected a portable telly in your room, so you can watch your favourite programmes until you fall asleep.'

'Yes, and I don't think I'll be long in doing that,' Louise said, stifling a yawn.

After Louise had gone to bed, Larry sat thinking over a large brandy about what he should do about the man named Steve, who must surely have been responsible for the death of his parents. Should he give the information he had to the police to follow or track him down and confront him, as Bottrell had suggested? He knew the right thing would be to report what he knew to the police, but he felt inclined to find the man himself first and see what he had to say. Yes, that's what I'll do, he thought. He'd go to his father's local pub at the first opportunity and see if he could find the man called Steve, who fitted faulty gas boilers.

CHAPTER FIVE

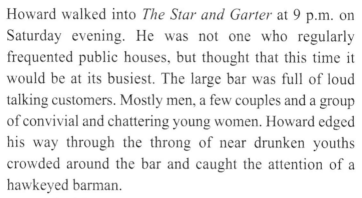

Howard walked into *The Star and Garter* at 9 p.m. on Saturday evening. He was not one who regularly frequented public houses, but thought that this time it would be at its busiest. The large bar was full of loud talking customers. Mostly men, a few couples and a group of convivial and chattering young women. Howard edged his way through the throng of near drunken youths crowded around the bar and caught the attention of a hawkeyed barman.

'A double Hennessey,' he ordered in a voice loud enough to be heard above the raucous din around the bar. The barman looked puzzled. 'A what?' he shouted.

Howard said in a loud clear voice: 'A first class VSOP cognac! You do sell cognac, don't you?'

The barman nodded. 'We just don't get much call for it here,' he said. He went to the shelves at the back of the bar and took several minutes locating a dust-covered bottle that contained brandy. He produced a brandy balloon and poured the drink.

Howard passed a ten-pound note over the bar. 'Take what it costs your fancy out of that, landlord.'

The barman put on a surprised look. 'Thanks guv, I'll have a Scotch on you, if that's okay,' he said placing the change on the bar.

Howard nodded assent. 'Put the change in the staff tronc,' he said, pushing the money back across the bar.

'Thanks a lot!' he said as he pocketed the cash. 'I wish all our new customers were as generous as you are, guv. I'll put it in the tip box later.'

'Yes, I have to admit I don't think I've ever visited this pub before. I suppose you know all your regulars.'

'Yes, I never forget a face, or a good tipper,' he replied with a broad grin.

'Just to test your knowledge of your customers, can you tell me if Steve is in here tonight?'

The barman looked thoughtful. 'Which Steve are you on about? I've got about three customers called Steve!'

'I'm sorry; I should be more precise. I think the Steve I want is a plumber.'

'Oh, you must mean Steve Capstick.' He gave a short laugh. 'I'm not sure about him being a plumber, but he does odd jobs and tries to turn his hand to most building work.'

'Yes, that sounds like the chap I'm looking for to do a job for me. Is he here now?'

'I don't know; he was in here earlier,' he replied, looking around the room. 'Yes, he's over in that far corner, next to the door with his son, Jack, and a couple of his cronies.'

'Thanks,' said Howard, moving away from the bar and making his way to within earshot of Capstick and his group.

'…the rozzers been to see you yet, Steve?'

'No, and I don't see why they should, Mike—I'm in the clear. My work was okay. The bloody gas leak must have come from one of the original supply pipes.'

'But didn't you fit a carbon monoxide alarm?' the other man asked.

Capstick gave a short laugh. 'No, Bert, when I asked the old geezer if he wanted one, he asked how much one would cost. When I quoted two hundred and forty quid to supply and fit one, he said, "I can't afford that much, I'm a pensioner. I'll get my son to do it for me." So it was all down to him!'

'Bloody hell, Steve, you certainly put a high price on your work. You can buy those bleedin' alarms for about thirty quid and they don't need much fitting—just a nail in the wall to hold it!'

Howard had heard enough. It was now clear that his mother and father had died because of the greed of this wretched man who stood just a few feet away. He felt an urge to take the man by the throat and choke him until his eyes popped out. However, the time was not right for a confrontation with Capstick. He needed to give the matter careful thought before he took any sort of action. But whatever he decided to do would need to be carried out in private.

Howard returned to the bar and caught the barman's eye. He beckoned him to the bar and, leaning forward, he almost whispered, 'Steve's too wrapped up with his friends, so I can't disturb him. Would you happen to know where he lives, so I can call on him about the work I want done?'

The barman nodded and went to the back of the bar and returned with a piece of paper and biro. He wrote the address on the paper and passed it to Howard.

Howard thanked him and left.

CHAPTER SIX

Two evenings later, Howard was watching a television series about *cowboy builders* and Louise was in bed reading. Howard had bought her a Kindle and to help replace her well- stocked library, destroyed in the fire, had downloaded about fifty novels, by her favourite authors, from Amazon.

The doorbell buzzed. He answered the door to see Bottrell standing in the corridor.

'I hope you don't mind me calling on you, Larry, but I feel so depressed over the death of my family and I thought a chat with you might help.'

'It's a bit late for callers, but if you think it might be some way to lift your depression, then come in, but I shan't want to stay up too late.'

Bottrell took off his raincoat and hung it on the hallstand before following Howard into the sitting room. He flopped down onto the chesterfield and looked at the television as Howard was about to turn it off.

'Oh... that's a coincidence... a programme about cowboy builders. Do you mind leaving it on, Larry? It might prove very interesting.'

'If you really want to see it, but I thought the subject would increase your depression. Anyway, it's nearly over,' said Howard, glancing at the mantel clock.

'Yes, Larry, but it'll keep me focussed on what I intend to do about Mr bleedin' Meldrum.'

'Meldrum? Is he the man who failed to fit a carbon monoxide alarm and is out on bail?'

'Yes, that's him—Reg Meldrum!'

'Well, at least the law has caught up with him. Gary and you can be assured that he'll probably receive a custodial sentence.'

'A custodial sentence! Huh… I bet he'll not do more than a couple of years!'

The programme ended and Howard switched off the television.

'Would you care for a drink, Gary? I bought a bottle of whisky yesterday. I don't know why. It might have been because you mentioned whisky when we first met.'

'Or you are a mind-reader and knew I'd be popping in to see you. Yes, I'd love one, Larry.'

Howard went to the sideboard and took out a bottle of whisky, a bottle of brandy and two appropriate glasses. He took the cap off the whisky bottle and pushed an optic into the top, then poured one measure of whisky into the highball glass. He handed it to the frowning Bottrell.

Bottrell took the glass. 'This is not a soldier's measure,' he said disdainfully. 'I'm not driving tonight, I came by taxi'

Howard gave a short humourless laugh. 'Okay, help

yourself,' he said, placing the whisky bottle on the sofa table in front of Bottrell.

Bottrell gave a sheepish look and poured a single measure into his glass. He's not very pleased with me—better sweeten him up, he thought. 'How's your sister coming along, Larry?'

'She's as well as can be expected, but it'll be quite some time before she's able to get back to work.'

'Where is she now—surely not out?' Bottrell didn't want anyone within earshot of what he wanted to discuss with Howard.

'No, she's tucked up in bed reading.'

Howard poured brandy into his glass and took a sip.

'Did you have any success in finding your cowboy builder, Larry?'

'Yes, I did. You were right about finding him in my father's local. I happened to hear him talking to his friends and from what I heard there's no doubt that his incompetence and greed resulted in the death of my parents.'

'What have you done about it?'

'Nothing yet—I'm still thinking about giving him a bloody good hiding before I pass what I know to the police.'

'The way things are these days, giving him a good hiding would get you into trouble. You could end up in clink yourself. What satisfaction is there for you in that?'

'Not a lot, I suppose; but the more I think about it the more I'd like to provoke him to fight me and then beat him to death, when there were no witnesses around. That might be worth being charged with manslaughter.'

'Hey, Larry, just a minute, you look pretty lightweight to me. Your man could be a real hard man and you could come out worse in the fight.'

Howard gave a short laugh. 'I know I don't look as though I could punch my way out of a wet paper sack, but I'm trained in the martial arts and take a class of students in the subject at the local gym.'

'Well, you do surprise me, Larry. I'd never have put you down as a tough guy. Between you and me, have you ever killed anyone?'

'You mean in war?'

'Of course!'

'That's something I don't normally talk about, Gary, but yes, I have killed—in self-defence! It happened when I was defusing an IED in Afghanistan. A couple of Taliban snipers kept me pinned down with little cover and took pot-shots at me. Fortunately they weren't very good marksmen and they didn't hit me or the IED. I feigned death and lay still as they came to loot my body of my personal possessions and collect my weapons and ammo. They talked and laughed excitedly as they neared me and didn't notice me easing my Colt automatic pistol out of its holster. They were a couple of yards away when I spun around to face them and loosed off two rounds at each of them. They were both dead before they hit the dirt!'

'I don't suppose you lost any sleep over that, did you?'

'No, it was them or me and we were at war.'

'So, given the right motivation, you are not against killing someone who has threatened your life or been the cause of killing a close relative or friend of yours?'

'Hmm… when you put it like that, I suppose I'm not. War cheapens life and can turn a meek-minded individual into a ruthless killer. But I'd need to be very strongly motivated to kill anyone, even in the circumstances you mentioned.'

Bottrell put on a very serious expression. 'Let me put this to you then—supposing someone offered, without any inducement or reward from you, to kill a person who had killed someone you loved?'

Howard sat up straight in his chair and snapped, 'Where are you going with all this talk about killing?'

Bottrell extended his arms. 'Simply this: I'm offering my services, with no strings attached, to deal with the man who caused the death of your parents and injury to your sister. Just give me his name and I'll be happy to oblige!'

Howard's eyebrows rose. 'Even if I agreed to what you have suggested, why would you do that for me?'

'You might find this difficult to accept, Larry, but I have developed a great respect for you. I also believe that in spite of the brave face you put on over the *virtual murder* of your parents, you are probably heartbroken by their death. I feel sure you know that if this case were to be brought to trial, the law would not mete out a punishment that would satisfy you that justice had been done.'

'Yes, I have to agree with what you say—but still, can't see why you would do that for me.'

'Then let me explain—supposing you took it into your head to kill this man, yourself. The police would investigate his death and they would eventually find out that he was the man who had been the cause of your parents' death. They'd straight away put you in the frame as the most likely suspect and keep ferreting away until they found evidence of your DNA on the victim. There would also be a problem for you in providing an acceptable alibi for the time of the death of the man. Believe me, Larry, I was in the Military Police and liaised with the civilian police and know their methods. Now, if I were to do away with your man I would have no connection with him or you so the police wouldn't come knocking on my door, and providing you had an alibi you'd be in the clear. Don't you see, Larry it's the one way you can avenge the death of your parents? So, why not let me have his name and address and I'll do the rest.'

Is this man completely bonkers or am I dreaming all this, thought Howard as he mulled over what Bottrell had suggested. What he says does make some sense, but I still can't see what there is in it for him. But… if he means what he says… why not take advantage of his offer?

'Well, Larry, I can see you're giving thought to what I have said. All I need is your man's name and address and for what he's been responsible for. I'll feel fully justified in making him suffer the extreme penalty.'

'Why not then?' Howard blurted out and reached for his wallet in his hip pocket. He took out the scrap of paper the barman had given him and dropped it on the table in front of Bottrell.

Bottrell picked up the paper and read out aloud: *Steve Capstick, 28 Marlborough Road, Woolwich.* He then slipped the paper into the top pocket of his jacket. 'That's it then, Larry. All I want you to do is to establish an iron-clad alibi when I telephone you that I am about to rid the world of Mr Steve Capstick.'

'Gary, if you do this for me it'll make me indebted to you for life. I have to say that I don't feel very comfortable with that sort of obligation hanging over my head. I shall have to make it up to you in some way in the future.'

'Larry, don't worry about that now. I'll think of something!'

'Then all I can say now is, take care and good luck.'

'That means there's nothing more to be said about this matter. Just a word of caution—above all, don't tell anyone, not even your sister, about our relationship. I'll let myself out—good night, Larry.'

'Good night, Gary.'

Bottrell walked the few hundred yards to the main road and caught a bus to take him to Deptford. Sitting in the nearly empty top deck of the bus he disconnected the tiny microphone from his jacket lapel and put it into the inside pocket of his jacket, where a miniature tape recorder had been recording his conversations with Howard.

After Bottrell had left, Howard sat drinking brandy and thinking about the agreement he had made with him. As much as he wanted to avenge the death of his parents, he began to think that he had been unwise in agreeing to Bottrell's offer. If he carried out his promise they would both be murderers. He must get in touch with him as soon as possible to stop him carrying out his promise. He'd give Capstick's address to the police and let the law take its laborious course in bringing him to justice. Then it occurred to him, Bottrell had been very vague about his address and place of work. He'd mentioned that he lived In Deptford and worked in some club in New Cross, but had not given his address, so he had no idea where Bottrell lived. He checked his telephone directories, which included Deptford, but there was no Gary Bottrell listed in any of them. I'll do some checking tomorrow and call at the police station in my lunch break, he decided. Draining his glass, he went to bed

CHAPTER SEVEN

At 7 a.m., next morning, Bottrell drove slowly past Capstick's house, noting the white van parked in the kerb, immediately opposite the house. The van bore the legend: *Something you need fixing? Then I'm your man—Ring 07099 666222 for the best service you'll get at a bargain price.* Bottrell smiled grimly, thinking that has to be Capstick's van.

He drove to Woolwich rail station and found a public telephone that was still operable and dialled the number he had seen on the van.

Almost immediately, a gruff voice answered, 'Hello?'

'Is that Mr Steve Capstick?'

'Yes, mate—who wants to know?'

'My name is Arthur Bainbridge, and your name has been recommended to me as someone who installs replacement gas boilers. I would like one replaced at the earliest opportunity. Would you be able to do this for me?'

'Of course I could—any time you like, Mr Bainbridge. Where's your house?

It's at Shooters Hill—it's not far from the pub at the top of the hill. I thought we could meet there. If you bring details with you of the types of gas boiler you recommend, we could have a drink and a spot of lunch while we talk over the job. When we've settled that I'll take you to my home to see where the boiler is to be fitted. Is that okay with you, Steve?'

There was a several seconds pause. Bottrell could almost hear Capstick thinking, *I've got a right berk here! He must be a bit of a toff, living on Shooters hill and taking me to lunch to talk about a job. I stand to make quite a bit out of this.* 'What time do you want to be at the pub?'

'Let's say at eleven o'clock. Is that all right for you, Steve?'

'Yes, I've nothing else on at the moment and can be there at eleven.'

'Good—I'll be sitting outside, so I can have a smoke while I wait for you.'

At 8.15 Bottrell rang the Greenwich Council offices and asked to be put through to the Clerk of Works' office.

'Larry Howard here, who's calling?'

'It's me,' Bottrell almost whispered.

'Oh, it's you. I'm really glad you rang. I wanted to contact you, but didn't have your address or telephone number. I've thought things over very carefully and have decided that I cannot agree to your proposal and want to cancel our arrangement.'

Bottrell sighed deeply. 'That's too bad, old chum, because the wheels are already in motion and there's no turning back now! What time do you go for your lunch break?'

Howard gulped noisily. 'I go to the canteen at about one o'clock.'

'Good, so you don't leave the building, then?'

'Yes, I do. I have to go out quite often to inspect building works.'

'In that case, put off your inspections until after lunch. But, from ten o'clock until midday, make sure that you are always in the presence of one of your colleagues or whoever else you might have dealings with. Do you understand?'

'Yes, I understand, but Gary, please listen to me we can't…'

There was a click at the other end of the line that told Howard the die was irrevocably cast.

* * * * *

At half-past ten Bottrell drove to the pub where he had arranged to meet Capstick and parked in a quiet side road, lined with trees, at the rear of the building. He walked round to the front of the pub, sat on the unoccupied bench outside, lit a cigarette and waited.

A few minutes before eleven Capstick arrived. Before he could get out of his cab, Bottrell got up from the bench and walked to the van. 'Don't get out Steve. I've changed my mind about having lunch here. We can go straight to the house and talk about boilers, while my wife makes us some sandwiches to go with a couple of cold beers. How does that suit you?'

Capstick nodded. 'That sounds great and it'll save a bit of time. I've got a top of the range boiler in the van so, if it's convenient for you, I could get on with the job this afternoon.'

'Splendid, just what I was hoping you'd say,' said Bottrell, climbing into the passenger seat next to Capstick.'

'Oh, I thought you'd be leading the way to your house in your car.'

'No, my car is in the local garage having a major service today. So, I'll direct you to my home—it's not very far from here.'

Capstick released the handbrake and the vehicle started to move slowly forward.

'Keep straight on over the hill, Steve. As a matter of interest, tell me, what mileage can you get to a litre of diesel with this van?'

Capstick laughed. 'I wouldn't get very far with diesel in my tank. I use petrol—and get about seven miles to the litre.'

'Do you see that large detached house about two hundred yards up the road on the right? Just make a right turn down the lane for about twenty yards and stop. My house is hidden behind some high bushes.'

Capstick followed Bottrell's directions and stopped the van. Turning to Bottrell with a look of puzzlement, he said: 'I can't see a house.'

'It's well covered by very high hedges,' retorted Bottrell. 'We get out here and walk a few yards to the footpath leading to the house.'

As Capstick turned to open the cab door, Bottrell drew a blackjack (which he had bought from an American military policeman) from his coat pocket and struck him twice across the back of his head. Capstick slumped forward in his seat and fell against the dashboard.

Bottrell quickly got out of the vehicle and went to the petrol cap. He unscrewed it and took a long white handkerchief from his top pocket. He twirled the handkerchief and lowered it into the tank. When it was soaked with petrol he pulled it halfway out and rested the petrol tank cap at an angle over it on the top of the input to the tank. Taking a box of matches from his pocket, he struck one and lit the corner of the exposed handkerchief and immediately ran to the row of trees and stood behind one. Within seconds, there was a tremendous explosion and the van became a blazing inferno. He watched behind the cover of the trees for a few seconds longer, then, seeing a man standing in the porch of the house on the opposite corner, he slipped away behind the cover of the trees to Shooters Hill. He walked briskly back down the hill to where his car was parked.

As he walked round the corner at the side of the pub a few people were beginning to come out of their houses to see where the explosion had occurred and two or three men were standing in the doorway of the pub pointing up the hill. He avoided their gaze and quietly and without haste drove away towards Plumstead. As he passed the fire station, a fire engine came roaring out and in the distance, he could hear the sirens of police cars and ambulances speeding towards the scene of the burning vehicle.

He took a different route back to Deptford and called in at a restaurant on the way for a hurried meal before he went home.

CHAPTER EIGHT

Detective Chief Inspector Ronald Hawksworth, a tall, grey haired, crime-weary detective, who was nearing retirement, tapped lightly on Chief Superintendent Ahmed Sharif's door. The Greenwich Borough Commander shouted, 'Come in!'

Hawksworth entered and Sharif gestured him to sit down.

'Well, what's the story on the exploding white van, Ron?' Sharif asked. He was a stickler for detail and insisted on being kept fully informed at all times with what was happening on his patch.

'There wasn't much left of it by the time we got there, boss. The van and the poor bugger driving it were burnt to a frazzle!'

'Has the driver been identified?'

'Yes, the registered number of the vehicle was passed to the DVLA and. they identified the vehicle as being owned by a Steve Capstick of 28 Marlborough Road, Woolwich.'

'Okay, but was Capstick driving the vehicle when it exploded?'

'Yes, we're 99 per cent sure about that. I sent DS Barry Loomis and a female officer to Capstick's house and his wife and son confirmed that he had driven the van away early that morning after he had received a call about a job. Loomis told Mrs Capstick about the accident and arranged for a family liaison officer to attend the family.'

'Is there anything known about Mr Capstick?'

'Yes, several minor traffic offences, a drunk and disorderly and one case of criminal assault. The Collator says he's a shifty individual who's probably been guilty of more serious offences, which as yet haven't come to our notice.'

'So, we should have his DNA on record then, Ron?'

'Yes, we have, which is just as well, because it would be nigh on impossible for anyone to identify what's left of him.'

'I take it you've arranged for a thorough inspection to be made of the vehicle and for an autopsy of this man's remains?'

'Yes, all that's in hand.'

'What about witnesses—were there any?'

'None have come forward. The van was a little out of sight of the houses, so it might not have been seen, but many people will have heard the explosion and come out of doors to see what had happened, which gives us the time it occurred. There were several people gawping at what was going on with the fire crew when we arrived, but none of them had actually seen the vehicle explode. Anyway, I arranged for a house-to-house check. But there were a few things that seemed rather odd.'

'Well, what were they?'

'The hand brake was on, so the vehicle was not moving when it exploded. This made me wonder why the driver didn't get out of the cab before the fire reached him? Another thing that I thought was odd was that the petrol cap was found several yards away from the vehicle and it was undamaged.'

'Hmm… so what are you suggesting, Ron, that this was not an accident?'

Hawksworth was well aware that the chief superintendent didn't put much faith in theories that couldn't be supported by hard evidence. 'Well, I think we ought to keep an open mind about the possibility that it wasn't an accident and that Capstick was murdered, boss.'

'Yes, what I find rather strange is why he was parked where he was. As I see it, there are two possibilities. His vehicle might have developed a malfunction and for some reason, which we are yet to discover, it caused the petrol tank to explode. On the other-hand, he could have stopped there to deliver something or to do a job at a nearby house. However, from what you said the vehicle was not directly outside any house. Send someone to check with the occupants of the nearest houses to find out if they were expecting anyone to call. Something else we need to know—in what sort of business was Capstick employed?'

'His wife told DS Loomis that her husband was a "jack of all trades" and could turn his hand to all sorts of building work. There was what remained of a gas boiler and all manner of tools in the back of the van, which seems to confirm what she said.'

'Now then, Ron, earlier you said that Mrs Capstick and her son had told DS Loomis that Capstick had received a call out to do a job. The fact that he was carrying a gas boiler suggests to me that he was going somewhere to fit that boiler.

'Yes, that's rather what I thought, boss.'

'I'm beginning to see that there is a lot more to this case that has not yet come to light. You can now look into all the matters we have discussed and put together a full report and have it on my desk first thing tomorrow morning. Oh, and something you've made no mention of—was a mobile phone found in the van or on Capstick? Because if there was we may be able to trace who made that call about a job.'

'Yes, we did find what was left of his mobile phone and it was found to be of no use at all, so I've sent it to the Forensic Laboratory to see what they can make of it,' Hawksworth smugly replied—determined not to be completely put down by his superior.

* * * * *

Bob Rutledge, a 28-year-old recently promoted detective inspector, was keen and ambitious to further his career, and was always eager to please his superiors by enthusiastically carrying out any task given to him. Today he was leading a section of police officers making a house-to-house check, a task he considered almost as boring as a fingertip search.

He started the ball rolling by calling at the large house nearest to where the van had exploded.

An elderly man, who had been dozing in a deckchair in the back garden, answered the door.

Before the man could speak, Rutledge flashed his warrant card across his face and said, unnecessarily loudly, 'Detective Inspector Rutledge, Greenwich CID. May I have your name, sir?'

The man blinked and took a step backward. 'Godfrey Truscott. What do you want?'

'I'm making enquiries into the explosion of a white van, which occurred near here earlier today. Did you hear or see anything?'

'Yes, at about eleven o'clock, when I was working in my garden at the back of the house. I heard a very loud explosion which reminded me of the V2 that dropped near here a few months before the war ended. Then a bit later I heard fire engines and police cars racing up Shooters Hill.'

Rutledge frowned. This was going to be difficult, he thought. 'Pray what is, or was, a V2, sir?' Not that he thought it was relevant, but he had to know.

Truscott looked at him as though he was explaining something to a backward schoolboy. 'It was a very large rocket which travelled faster than sound and was capable of knocking down a whole street of houses. If you heard the explosion, you knew you were alive. If you didn't you were probably dead!'

'That's all very interesting, sir, but did you see the van or anyone near it?'

'I came out and looked down the road. The fire crew were hosing water at the blazing vehicle, but the fire had too strong a hold on the vehicle and it couldn't be saved, so they let it burn out.'

'Yes, but did you see anyone near the burning vehicle?'

'Yes, I saw several police officers talking to the crowd of people, who were gathered near the vehicle.'

'Of course, I know you must have seen police and a crowd of gawping voyeurs, but what I want to know is, did you see anyone acting suspiciously or moving away from the scene in a car, on a bicycle or on foot?'

Truscott looked thoughtful and stroked his bearded chin before he answered. 'Yes, now you come to mention it, I did see a man standing near one of the trees and looking towards the burning vehicle.'

Rutledge's heart skipped a beat. 'Can you describe him?'

'Not really, I only saw him briefly. One moment he was there and then he wasn't. He must have gone through the trees, because I would have seen he if he had returned to the pathway.'

'Is there anything at all you can say about his appearance?'

'Only that he looked like a man and was wearing dark clothing, a suit, I think, but I'm afraid that's all I can remember.'

I'd be flogging a dead horse to question this man any more, thought Rutledge. 'Thank you, sir. You have been most helpful,' he lied, believing the man to be a *Times* reader who might write to the commissioner if he considered a police officer had been discourteous to him.

When Rutledge and his team had completed their house-to-house check they went to Woolwich police station to be debriefed by DCI Hawksworth.

'Well, was it worth the trouble, Bob?'

'Not really, I've questioned the team and none of them gleaned any useful information from the residents in the area. But I think I prevented it being a complete waste of police time, guv, because an old codger I questioned said that he had seen a man observing the burning vehicle from behind a tree.'

'Hmm... that does seem a tad suspicious. Did you get a description of the man, if it was a man?'

'He said that it was a man dressed in dark clothing, probably a suit.'

'Well, I suppose that's something to go on then. Put all you and the team have got into a report and let me have it ASAP. The chief wants a progress report first thing in the morning.'

* * * * *

At eight o'clock next morning, DCI Hawksworth placed DI Rutledge's report on Chief Superintendent Sharif's desk.

'I'm afraid what we've found out so far doesn't provide us with very much to go on, sir.'

Sharif quickly read the two-page report. 'No, you're right about that, Ron! The only significant piece of information is Rutledge's man in a dark suit, briefly watching the burning vehicle from behind a tree. What do you make of that?'

'Hawksworth gave a slight shrug of his shoulders. 'Not a lot, but I ask myself, why he hid behind a tree to watch the blaze. He'd have got a much better view by standing in the road. And then there's the dark suit he was wearing. That suggests to me that he wasn't a local to be dressed like that, at eleven in the morning. He was visiting someone. But how did he get there? If it were by car, he would surely have driven straight to the house he was visiting. One thing we did get from the residents is that no one had seen a car parked anywhere near where the explosion occurred. Now, if the man had been a sales representative or some sort of canvasser he would surely have had a vehicle to carry his goods or other materials. There is a bus service that serves Shooters Hill, but that's most unlikely to be used by sales people or canvassers.'

Sharif leaned forward over his desk and looked knowingly at Hawksworth. 'You can stop there, Ron and listen. What do you think about this as an answer to the question of how he got there? I suggest that he could have been a passenger in the van!'

'That had crossed my mind, boss, but I thought you'd dismiss it as an unsupported theory.'

'That's where you are wrong, Ron. Remember what DS Loomis said about what he'd learnt from Mrs Capstick and her son. They said that Capstick had received a phone call early that morning and had gone out to meet someone about a job. Now if the man who phoned him is the same man who I believe was a passenger in the van, then I think we've got a good lead to finding Capstick's killer. Do you agree?'

'I can go along with your reasoning, but if what you say is correct, this murder, if it was murder, was very carefully planned by someone who must have had a very strong motive to kill Capstick in the way he did.'

Sharif smiled, something he rarely did. 'I'm glad to see that your ageing brain is now in top gear, Ron. Another question answered—the reason why Capstick didn't leave his cab as soon as the vehicle exploded can now be explained. His passenger either stunned him or killed him before he left the vehicle and set alight the petrol tank, then quickly took cover behind a tree to watch his handiwork. So, what we've got to do is to find the man who hated Capstick enough to do away with him in the way he did. Off you go then, Ron, and keep me informed of your progress.'

Hawksworth was glad to leave Sharif; an audience with him was like reporting to the headmaster's office to receive six of the best. His first priority now was to plan how he was going to direct his detectives in the search for the suspected murderer that Sharif had produced as a conjurer does when he takes an egg from an empty bag.

* * * * *

DS Eddie Parsons, DC Derek Holmes and DC Terri Burnside gathered in Hawksworth's office to receive a briefing on the lines of enquiry they should follow.

He addressed Terri, an attractive young woman, who in her short time with CID had developed a successful technique in interviewing traumatized victims of crime and their families. 'I want you to accompany the Families Liaison Officer to interview Mrs Capstick and her son. What I want to know is exactly what Capstick said to the person who telephoned him at his home yesterday morning. Also, try to find out the names of any of his friends and workmates. Report anything you learn to DS Parsons. Off you go then.'

Terri gathered up her handbag and notebook and left the office.

'Derek, have a word with the pathologist who examined Capstick's remains. Ask him if he found any signs of violence on the body. Particularly any head wounds.

'Without referring to Capstick's family, Eddie, question their neighbours and customers of local pubs about Capstick. Try to find out if he had any enemies or customers, who were disgruntled enough with his services to go as far as killing him. If any names come up, let me know straight away. Check with Terri and Gary from time to time and let me have anything they may have gleaned from their enquiries.'

DS Parsons called at all of Capstick's nearest neighbours. Each time he asked if they were aware of anyone who might bear a grudge against him. Although no one provided any information concerning possible enemies of Capstick, it became clear that he was not a very popular member of the neighbourhood.

Parsons did learn where Capstick spent his leisure time. Usually in the *Star and Garter* with one or two, equally, unpopular casual workers named Bert and Mike, who were unemployed but always seemed to have enough money to spend and add to the extended lunch hours in the pub.

Parsons went into a café a few yards from the pub and sat drinking coffee until noon, when he reckoned regulars would be gathering in the pub.

He entered the pub at a few minutes past midday, ordered a pint of bitter and sat down within earshot of a group of loud-mouthed drinkers. Hoping to hear the name Bert or Mike mentioned, he listened carefully to everything said until he had finished his drink, then went to the bar to order another.

'Just make it a half this time. I was supposed to meet a couple of chaps in here. Would you happen to know if Mike and Bert have been in today?'

The barman shook his head. 'Sorry mate; I've only worked here for a couple of weeks and don't know many of the customers by name. If the head barman, who knows all the customers by name, had been here, he would have been able to tell you, but it's his day off today.'

Parsons thanked him and took his beer to the other side of the bar. As he went to sit at a corner table four men entered the pub arguing about who should buy the first round. 'It's your turn, Bert!' one almost shouted. Bert sidled up to the bar and ordered, 'Four pints of bitter,' while his three companions sat at the table next to Parsons.

Returning with the tray of glasses, Bert joined the others. There were only four chairs around the table and Parsons occupied one. Bert placed the tray on the table and glared at Parsons.

'It's okay, Bert,' Parsons said with a forced smile, 'I'll move onto the bench seat so you can join your pals.'

Bert looked puzzled by a stranger's use of his name, but said nothing and sat down in Parsons' vacated chair.

'Well, I suppose we'd better make a toast, or something, to our newly departed drinking mate,' said one of the men.

'Yeah, Fred, Old Steve's life was full of ups and downs, but there's no doubt about it, he certainly went out in a blaze of glory!' Bert said with a laugh, then raising his glass he gulped down half of his beer.

The others followed suit.

'But that was a bloody awful way to go out—burnt to a crisp, because he couldn't get out of his cab quick enough,' Fred said.

Parsons couldn't believe his luck. He had four of Capstick's drinking mates sitting next to him and talking about Capstick's *accident*. He had, somehow, to join their conversation.

'Mind you, I have my doubts that it was an accident,' said one of the men, who hadn't spoken before. 'He fiddled enough people in his time to have made enemies, who might have been pleased to see him roast in Hell.'

'You could be right there, George,' Fred said. 'Only last week he fitted a gas boiler in a house, not far from here. There was a leak in a gas pipe and the house blew up killing an old couple and injuring their daughter. It was down to Steve, because he didn't check for gas leaks or fit an alarm.'

Parsons leant forward. 'Excuse me gents, but I couldn't help hearing what you said about the house that exploded. From what you said about your late friend, Steve, it's very likely that had he survived his accident he would have been charged with manslaughter. I heard from a friend, a reporter for the *Greenwich Herald*, that the police were trying to trace the man who had installed the boiler.'

'I'm not surprised,' replied Fred. 'They must think that Steve was probably murdered by a member of the family of the old couple, who were killed by the explosion.'

It gets better and better, thought Parsons. He now remembered the case, and what these men had said seemed to support the possibility of criminal negligence of the gas boiler fitter. He decided that it was time for him to leave and report to the DCI.

'Gentlemen, I hope you didn't mind me joining in your conversation, but I found it very interesting. I see that you are all ready for another drink. Please let me pay for it.' Parsons put a ten-pound note in the middle of the table.

'Thanks mate,' the group shouted in chorus, 'you're a star!'

Parsons laughed and gave a little wave as he walked out of the pub. He couldn't wait to get back to his station to report what he had heard. The information he had must surely be worth a few Brownie points towards promotion to detective inspector, he thought.

CHAPTER NINE

Larry Howard and Louise were watching an evening news programme when the doorbell buzzed

'Who can that be at this time of night?' Louise said, startled.

'I don't know, I'm not expecting anyone. But we'll not find out unless I answer the door,' Howard replied with a broad grin. 'It's probably just someone trying to sell something.'

Howard opened the door to see two stern-faced men standing in the passage. Certainly not salesmen, he thought, they always have smiling faces.

The elder looking of the pair produced a card and flashed it in front of Howard's face. 'I'm Detective Inspector Rutledge and my colleague is Detective Constable Holmes, of Greenwich CID. Are you Laurence Howard?'

'Yes, I am,' replied Howard in as cool a voice as he could muster.

'May we come in, sir? We have questions we need to ask you regarding the death of your parents.'

'Certainly, come in gentlemen. I hope you have found

the man who was responsible for the explosion that caused their deaths.'

Rutledge didn't reply as he and Holmes followed Howard into the sitting room.

'We've got a visit from the law, Louise. They've found the man who was responsible for the explosion.'

'Are they going to prosecute him?'

Before Howard could reply, Rutledge said: 'From the sling you are wearing, I take it you are Louise Howard, who was injured in the explosion?'

'Yes, Inspector, Louise is my sister, and she was about to go to bed before you arrived,' Howard replied before Louise could answer.

Louise looked questioningly at her brother, but didn't contradict him. She knew that he must have had a good reason for her to leave the room. 'Goodnight, Larry,' she said as she rose from the sofa.

'Goodnight, Louise. Don't forget you've got a hospital appointment at 10 a.m. tomorrow. I'll give you an early call and we'll have breakfast together before I leave for work,' Larry said as Louise left the room.

'That's rather a pity,' said Rutledge with a frown. 'I would have liked your sister to have been present when I questioned you.'

'Questioned me? I thought you had come here this evening to tell us that you'd found the man responsible for our parents' deaths?'

'We might have, sir,' Rutledge replied, with a faint smile.

'Then please be seated and fire away with your questions, Inspector.'

The detectives sat on the sofa. Holmes produced a notebook and a pen, and Rutledge looked intently at Howard.

Rutledge cleared his throat before he spoke. 'Steven Capstick, the man who fitted the replacement gas boiler in your parents' home, has been found dead and it is necessary to question everyone involved in this case.'

'I don't understand why you should have reason to think that I am *involved* in any way with this man's death.'

Rutledge frowned before he answered. 'The fact is, Mr Howard, that there is every reason to believe that Capstick was murdered. Therefore, it is very necessary to question everyone who had any connection with him.'

'Then, I suggest that you are wasting your time by questioning me, because apart from what you have just told me, I know nothing about this man!'

Rutledge glanced sideways at Holmes, who scribbled something in his notebook.

'That may be so, but there is one question I must ask you. Where were you between the hours of ten and eleven last Thursday?'

Howard scratched his neck and pretended to think before he answered. 'I would have been in my office at the Greenwich Council building.'

'Is there anyone who can corroborate that you were there?'

Howard screwed up his face in false concentration.

'Yes—about that time I was in discussion with my manager.'

Holmes scribbled some more.

'What is the name of your manager?'

'Geoffrey Mounsell.'

'Are quite sure you weren't on Shooters Hill at that time?'

'Yes, I'm positive that I was in Geoff Mounsell's office most of that morning.'

'That's good, but I shall have to speak to your manager before we can eliminate you from our inquiries.'

'Yes, I quite understand, Inspector; you have to be very thorough in your job,' Howard said in a deliberately patronising tone. 'Have you any more questions for me?'

'No, Mr Howard, not at this this time, but we may have to see you again.'

'Then I'll bid you good night, Inspector, Constable,' said Howard as he led them to the door.

CHAPTER TEN

The morning after the police visit, Larry and Louise were having an early breakfast while watching the television news.

'Tell me, Larry, why did you send me to bed when those detectives came here last night?'

Howard stopped spreading marmalade on a slice of toast before he answered. 'The fact of the matter is, I thought you had heard enough about the *accident* and, anyway, you needed a good night's rest before attending your hospital appointment this morning.'

'That was very considerate of you, but I'm just as interested as you are to learn how the police investigation is progressing. Have they arrested that man Steve yet?'

'No, they told me that he had been found dead in his van.'

'Oh! How very odd. Had he committed suicide, or just died of natural causes?'

'No, they told me that his van had caught fire and burnt him to death.'

'How awful! But I can't say I feel very sorry about that. It would seem he got his just deserts! But it's rather strange that two policemen would come here late in the evening to tell you about it. Is that all they had to say?'

'Yes, more or less, but—'

The ringing of the telephone silenced Larry. He sat listening to the persistent ring, knowing it had to be Bottrell.

'Aren't you going to answer it, Larry?'

'Yes, of course, I was just wondering who would call us so early in the morning,' he replied as he went to answer the telephone.

'Hello.'

'It's me, Larry. We must meet; we have much to talk about.'

'I know, but it's not convenient at the moment—I'm just about to leave for the office.'

'Okay—let's meet at the coffee shop next to the British Home Stores in Greenwich at 12.30. Is that all right for you?'

'Yes, I'll be there,' Larry replied and replaced the receiver.

'You were a bit short with whoever that was, Larry. Anyway, who was it?'

'Oh… nobody you know. Just a chap I knew in the army, who wants some advice about getting planning permission to build a conservatory on to his house.'

'Huh, he wasn't being very considerate ringing at this time in the morning! You should have told him to call at your office or telephone you there,'

'Yes, I suppose I should have, but he's only recently

left the army and isn't yet accustomed to how things are done in civil life. Hey, I've no time for any more small talk. I must be off. I'll see you this evening. I hope all goes well for you at the hospital. Do you need any money for taxi fares?'

'No thanks, I've still got some of the money you gave me for shopping. See you this evening and anyway I've plenty of money in the bank if I need it.'

Howard drained his teacup and left the table. 'Cheerio and take care,' he said as he went into the hall to collect his topcoat.

After he left Louise sat drinking tea, she thought: *I have the distinct feeling that there is something going on he doesn't want me to know about.*

* * * * *

Bottrell was sitting in the far corner of the coffee shop when Howard arrived. He joined him and sat down at the table.

Howard glared at Bottrell until a waitress came to the table.

'What's it to be?' she asked.

'An Americano,' said Howard without taking his gaze from Bottrell.

'Make that two, sweetie,' Bottrell added.

'That was a stupid thing to do, telephoning me at my flat. I couldn't talk with Louise sitting next to me. Anyway, why did you ring me at all?'

'Haven't you heard, Larry? Steve Capstick went out

in a blaze of ignominy and we have some further business to discuss.'

'Yes, I have, the police came to see me last night to tell me and I've seen a report in the local paper, about him being burnt in his van.'

Bottrell gave a little laugh, but didn't speak until the waitress had placed their coffees on the table and left. 'I bet the police asked you where you were last Thursday.'

'Yes, they did. But this was a damned silly place to meet for whatever you wanted to talk about. This café is used by a lot of the Council staff and being seen with you could prove to be a dangerous link.'

Bottrell finished his coffee before he replied. 'So where would you like us to meet?'

Howard gave a little shrug. 'What do you want to talk about?'

Bottrell's eyes blazed. 'Stop playing games with me, Larry, you know damn well what you now have to do to level the score!'

'You mean you really expect me to do away with your Mr Meldrum?'

'I sure do! That was the plan as far as I am concerned. So, you'd better get your finger out and let me know when, where and how you intend carrying out your side of the bargain. I need that information to create an alibi.'

Howard gravely shook his head from side-to-side. 'No, I have no intention of committing murder, whatever the circumstances. I tried to stop you taking action against Capstick, but was unable to contact you in time. Now let's be sensible about this, put it all behind us and not meet again. After all we did have rather a lot to drink the evening you put the suggestion to me.'

Bottrell's eyes narrowed to slits. 'Yes, I'm sure you'd like to do that. I've put myself at great risk carrying out revenge for you. Now it's your turn, and before you say another word I have to tell you that I have your agreement to terminate Meldrum recorded and if you refuse to carry out our agreed plan I shall pass it to the police.'

'Huh, wouldn't that reveal to the police your part in the plan?'

'Possibly, but I'd make sure I wasn't around to be nicked. I have an alternative plan, which wouldn't involve the police. I'm sure you wouldn't want your dear sister to know what you had agreed to do.'

'No, I wouldn't and I beg you not to involve her in any way.'

'You're softening up, Larry. You must now see that the only way our talk will remain a secret just between us, is for you to carry out what you agreed to do.'

'All, right, damn you! I'll do what you want, but I need time to plan the operation.'

'*Plan the operation*! Don't give me all that military crap! Meldrum is up before the court next week and will almost certainly be found guilty and sent down for a couple of years. Once he's in the nick we'll have lost our chance to get him. You've got at most four days to see that he never gets to court. If the job's not done by the time I'll go public. So, you'd better piss off to your little flat and start *planning the operation* right away! And when you come up with a plan, let me know.'

Howard just nodded and said, with a tinge of sarcasm in his tone, 'Okay, Chief!'

Bottrell got up from the table. 'Cheerio for now, Larry; do keep in touch; you know what I want to hear. I'm sure you made a note of my mobile number when I rang you at home and here's Meldrum's address and telephone number. He lives on his own in a two up and two down terrace house.' He dropped a piece of paper on the table in front of Howard and then walked out of the café, leaving Howard to pay for their coffee.

Howard slipped the piece of paper into his inside jacket pocket, placed a five-pound note under his saucer, waited for a couple of minutes and then walked out of the café and back to his office.

He cleared what he could from his in-tray and then went to his line manager's office. 'Geoff, I'm afraid I need a few more days leave. Louise still needs my attention until she's fit enough to return to work and there are the arrangements to be made for the funeral of my parents, plus dealing with the insurance companies involved.'

'I quite understand what you've got to deal with, Larry. I always thought that you came back to work far too early. You take what time off you need. You've had no other time off this year.'

'Thanks, Geoff, that's certainly taken a load off my mind. If I have to extend my absence, I can always apply for unpaid leave. I'll brief Sid Prentice on any outstanding work that will need urgent attention while I'm away.'

'Yes, of course you can, Larry, and don't worry about what's in your pending tray; the rest of your team can cope with that—no one is indispensable. Now off you go and deal with what you have to.'

Little does he know of what I have to deal with, thought Howard as he left the office.

Before returning home, Howard went to a shop, which supplied masks, disguises and fancy dress costumes. Louise had told him about the shop when she'd bought items for use in school plays and fancy dress balls she had attended. He bought a false moustache and beard, some horn-rimmed spectacles. Next, he went to a charity shop and bought an ancient, but still serviceable, 1940s raglan style raincoat and a tweed cap.

He arrived home to find that Louise had not returned from her hospital appointment. Just as well, he thought. She'd want to know what he had in the large carrier bag. He placed the bag behind his overcoat in the bottom of his wardrobe.

After making himself a sandwich and a cup of coffee, he collected his disguise outfit from the wardrobe and put it next to the driver's seat. He would have preferred to change into his disguise in the flat, but that would have required some outlandish explanation if Louise had suddenly come back from wherever she was. He drove to Blackheath rail station, where he knew there was one of the few remaining public telephones in the village. He dialled Meldrum's mobile phone number. It was answered immediately.

'Hello, who's that?' a coarse voice asked.

'Is that Mr Hardwick?' asked Howard in a Sloan Square accent.

'No, it bloody isn't!' Meldrum shouted and slammed the phone down.

That sounds like it might be Meldrum and he's in. I just hope he's alone.

Next he dialled Bottrell's number. There was a delay of a minute before he answered.

'Who's that?' Bottrell asked in a breathless voice.

He's obviously entertaining one of his sleazy nightclub girls, thought Howard. 'I'm just calling to let you know that the performance you don't want to miss is on this evening. I hope you will enjoy it.' Howard said this in his best imitation of Michael Caine's accent and put down the phone.

Bottrell, standing naked beside the bed with the phone in his hand, turned to his companion for the evening. 'Get yourself up my dear; we're going to the theatre.'

Howard drove into the car park next to the station and quickly put on his disguise. He then drove to Meldrum's address and parked about twenty yards past Meldrum's house. He walked back to house. There was a small white van parked at the front of the house. He noticed that there was a chink of light showing between the drawn curtains of the front room. He rang the doorbell. A minute passed before a light came on in the hall and the front door opened to reveal a short, scrawny, middle-aged man, dressed in jeans and a check shirt with the sleeves rolled up.

'Good evening Mr Meldrum. I hope I'm not disturbing you, but—'

'Yes, you bloody well are—what do you want?'

'I'm very sorry to have disturbed you, but I am in need of some urgent plumbing work to be done in my house and your name has been recommended to me by a chap I met in a pub.'

'What was the chap's name?'

'Oh… Fred… Mike… I can't remember. But he said he was in the plumbing business but had too much work on to help me at present and referred me to you.'

'What do you want done?'

'I want a small gas-fired boiler fitted. It's not a big job, but I want it done as soon as possible and am prepared to pay for the work in cash. I have all the details about the boiler with me, but it will have to be purchased from a wholesaler.'

'Okay, you'd better come in.'

Meldrum led Howard into the sitting room.

'What's your name and address, mate?'

'My name is Lionel Blyton and if it is convenient for you I can drive you to my home this evening to show you where I want the boiler fitted,' said Howard, handing Meldrum a leaflet about gas boilers, which he had picked up from a local DIY shop that day. The one he had chosen was marked with a cross.

Meldrum gave a cursory glance at the leaflet. 'Oh, yes, I know all about this model. It'll be no problem to fit it, but I'll need cash up front to buy it and cover incidental expenses.'

'That's splendid. I'm quite happy to pay in advance for your work, if you can get it done tomorrow.'

'Good, so let's go and see where you want it fitted. Hang on a minute while I get my coat,' Meldrum said as he turned to leave the room.

Howard stepped in front of Meldrum and delivered a savage judo blow to his larynx. Meldrum fell to the floor. Howard checked his pulse; there was none, he was dead.

Howard put on surgical rubber gloves, turned off the television and pulled a twenty-foot length of clothesline from his raincoat pocket. He made a noose at one end of the rope and slipped it over Meldrum's head. Next, he lifted Meldrum off the floor and carried him out to the passage and up the stairs to the landing. He leant Meldrum up against the bannisters and looped the rope over the bannister rail, which he estimated was about fifteen feet above the passage floor. Meldrum was about five-feet six, so he loosened the rope up to seven-foot six, This, he considered, would mean that Meldrum's feet would reach about two feet from the floor, high enough to accommodate a chair under his hanging feet. He tightly wound the spare rope around his waist and then lifted Meldrum on top of the banister rail and pushed him over. There was a loud cracking noise as Meldrum's neck was broken. Howard unwound the rope from his waist and knotted it securely around the bannister rail. He went downstairs,   took a dining chair from the kitchen and pushed it over near Meldrum's hanging feet.

Howard inspected the stairs, landing and sitting room

to see if there were any traces of him having been in the house. As far as he could ascertain there were none. He turned off all the downstairs lights, but left the landing light on. He stood behind the front door to listen for passing traffic or pedestrians. When all was quiet outside, he opened the front door, stepped outside and closed it noiselessly. He returned to his car, drove off and returned to Blackheath. When he arrived at his normal parking spot, he took off his disguise, put it in the carrier bag and placed it in the car boot.

When he entered his flat, he found that Louise was lying on the sofa watching television.

'I'm glad to see you're back from the hospital, I was beginning to worry,' he said, thinking it the right thing to say.

'No, I wasn't there very long. The consultant cleared me to go back to work next week, so I called in to the school to tell the head teacher. I did try to let you know where I was, but you must have been out. Where were you this evening?'

'Oh... I er... just called in to see Geoff Mounsell about some job and we got talking about various things. You know how it is. Now I just feel like a drink of hot chocolate and an early night.'

Louise yawned. 'Yes, I know how it is when two men start to chat about work. I think I'll join you in having hot chocolate, if you're making it, and getting an early night,' Louise said as she turned off the television.

CHAPTER ELEVEN

PC Dodsworth stopped his police patrol car at the kerb, behind the white van parked outside 8 Farley Terrace. 'This is Meldrum's address, Pete,' he said to his companion, PC Danby.

They both got out of the vehicle and walked to the front door. Dodsworth rang the bell. There was no answer.

'He must be out,' suggested Danby.

'Yes, it looks that way. But this is his van,' replied Dodsworth. 'I checked its registered number before I left the station.'

'Shall I radio in and let the duty inspector know he's not here, Mike?' said Danby, who was a probationer constable who was always anxious to exercise his initiative.

'No, not yet, Pete, I've got a gut feeling that there's something very amiss here. Look, the curtains are still drawn at this time of the afternoon. And his van's here, so if he's out he's not gone very far.'

'What do we do then?'

'We'll check with his immediate neighbours to see if they've seen him today.'

Dodsworth rang the bell at number10. A middle-aged woman in hair curlers and dressed in a floral pinafore almost immediately opened the door. As an active member of the local Neighbourhood Watch Scheme, she had been looking out of the window to see who was stopping outside her house. Seeing two police officers, she was keen to know what was happening in her street.

'Good morning, madam, sorry to disturb you but we're trying to contact Mr Meldrum, your next door neighbour,' said Dodsworth. 'Have you seen him this morning?'

'No, I haven't seen him for three or four days. He can't have been out working because his van's not been moved for days. My husband told me that he'd heard that Mr Meldrum had been summoned to go to court today.'

Dodsworth didn't confirm her information. 'What is your name, please?'

'Mrs Kate Frisby, I'm the deputy neighbourhood co-ordinator for this street,' the woman replied.

'Thank you very much, Mrs Frisby, you've been a great help,' said Dodsworth with a smile.

Mrs Frisby remained at her door and watched the two officers.

'Do you think he's still in the house and hiding, Mike?'

'No, Pete, if he's still in the house, I'd bet he's dead!'

'What makes you think that, Mike?'

'From my experience, Pete, persons having to appear in court on a serious charge, which may result in them being sentenced to imprisonment, can, sometimes, cause them to commit suicide.'

'So, you think he's dead in there?'

'I think it's a strong possibility that he is.'

'So, what do we do now?'

'We gain entrance, of course, but looking at that door, I think it'll have to be a window. One at the back of the house might be the best way.'

Mrs Frisby, who had heard most of what Dodsworth and Danby had been saying, came out of her porch and called to them: 'I say, if you want to get into Mr Meldrum's house without busting his front door down, you can come through mine to get around the back. You might find that his back door's not locked.'

'Yes, that would be a help, Mrs Frisby. Pete, you stay in the car ready to report what I find inside.'

Dodsworth followed Mrs Frisby into her house and out to the back garden. There was a four-foot fence between the back gardens. Dodsworth clambered over it and went to the back door; it was locked, but he soon opened the door by kicking it at the side of the doorknob. He entered the kitchen and immediately became aware of the unmistakable smell of death. He went into the hall and the smell grew stronger. The cause became apparent—it was the decomposing body of Meldrum, hanging from the bannisters, surrounded by a swarm of flies.

Dodsworth opened the front door, joined Danby in the car and told him to report that he had found a dead body in Meldrum's house. Within a few minutes, a convoy of police vehicles arrived carrying the duty detective inspector, two detective sergeants and several detective constables, a forensic pathologist, a scenes-of-crime team and the coroner's officer. Meldrum's house was cordoned off and a full-scale investigation began.

* * * * *

'Has the identity of the man found hanged in Meldrum's flat been established,Ron?' Chief Superintendent Ahmed Sharif asked Detective Chief Inspector Ronald Hawksworth.

'Well, not by a relative. He doesn't seem to have any in the area. But a close neighbour, who is an active member of the local neighbourhood watch scheme, says she's sure the body is that of Meldrum.'

'Has anything else filtered through from the scene yet?'

'An initial examination of the body suggests that Meldrum committed suicide by hanging himself, sir.'

'Is there anything known about the deceased?'

'Yes, our collator's records show that he is suspected of some sharp practises in his work as a general "jack of all trades" in the building industry. What some would call a "cowboy builder" but we had nothing to nail him until we got him on the manslaughter charge, for which he should have attended Woolwich Crown Court this morning.'

'Cowboy builder, eh? I've always thought that a rather odd name to give an incompetent tradesman. I used to enjoy cowboy films when I was a young boy. I seem to remember that the goodies always wore white hats and the baddies wore black ones. But I'm sorry, I digress,' said Sharif with an almost soundless laugh.

'Yes, thinking about it, I'm inclined to agree with you, sir.'

'Ron, I have to say, I'm not very happy with the way DI Rutledge manages his section. I think you'd better take over the investigation and keep me fully informed of all developments.'

'But sir, everything indicates that this is simply a case of suicide by a man who couldn't face the possibility of a prison sentence. With regard to Rutledge, he's only recently been promoted on transfer to this borough. He naturally lacks experience in his new rank, but he is an enthusiastic officer who does his level best whatever the circumstances.'

'Rutledge aside, Ron, I'm not convinced, from what I've heard, that this is a simple case of suicide. Has a suicide note been found?'

'Not yet, but then they're not always written.'

'That's true, but mean-minded crooks like Meldrum don't usually have a conscience strong enough to take their own life because they've been responsible for the death of others. Anyway, get yourself over there and dig a bit deeper. I feel there's more to this case than meets the eye.'

* * * * *

Two days later, at 10 a.m., Chief Superintendent Sharif was chairing a meeting in his office. In attendance were his deputy, Superintendent Lauren Armitage, DCI Ron Hawksworth, DI Bob Rutledge, DS Barry Loomis and DS Edward Parsons to discuss the implications arising from the pathologist's report on the post mortem examination of Reginald Meldrum.

Sharif opened the meeting. 'You have all seen the pathologist's report on the autopsy of Meldrum. His findings make it quite clear that we have a murder on our hands and not a *simple case of suicide,* as some of us thought, or wished to be the case. Meldrum's neck was broken when he went over the banisters, but he was already dead when that happened because an extremely heavy blow had crushed his larynx. Commandos are trained to use this blow to kill enemy sentries silently. So, this was a premeditated and well-planned murder. This reminds me of a similar murder made to look like suicide, which I read somewhere in the past. It happened in West Germany in the early fifties and involved two British army sergeants, friends, but during a heated argument one struck the other in the larynx and killed him. He then strung him up to make it look as though his victim had committed suicide, by hanging himself. But all that aside, Ron, can you add anything to what I've said that might throw further light on the sort of person we're looking for?'

'Well, sir, if we're are looking for a suspect, we might well start with Gary Bottrell, the man whose wife and young daughter were killed by carbon monoxide poisoning. Meldrum had fitted a new gas boiler in Mrs Bottrell's house, but had not checked for leaks from the pipework, nor had he fitted a safety alarm. Therefore, the victims were not alerted to the escape of the deadly fumes. Meldrum was arrested and charged with manslaughter, he was remanded for trial in the Woolwich Crown Court and should have appeared there three days ago.'

'Yes, I suppose, from what you say, Bottrell had a very strong motive to mete out his own form of justice. What do we know about this man?'

Hawksworth rose and said: 'As soon as I saw the pathologist's report, I had a check run on Bottrell. He is a 35-year-old ex-soldier—a corporal in the Royal Military Police. He was described as a rather brutish individual. I learned from the military authorities that five years ago Bottrell was charged with causing grievous bodily harm to a young soldier who was in his custody. He was court-martialled, found guilty, stripped of his rank, sentenced to 56 days detention and dishonourably discharged from the Army. Since then he has been employed as a bouncer in a sleazy gambling club in New Cross.'

'It seems we need to look no further for Meldrum's killer. As a military police NCO, it's quite possible that he may have been trained to kill in the way that the pathologist has reported. Has he been questioned, arrested, in custody, or now fled the country?' Sharif said with a trace of sarcasm in his tone.

Hawksworth's face reddened. 'I instructed DI Rutledge to bring him in for questioning, but thought that we should wait until you had ruled on the matter.'

'Then away you go, Rutledge, and bring him in before he flits. He sounds like he might be a bit of a handful, so take a DC with you.'

'Yes, sir, I'm off!' Rutledge jumped up and almost ran out of the chief superintendent's office.

* * * * *

DI Rutledge, accompanied by DC Joe Madden, a hard-bitten copper of 26 years' service, drove to Bottrell's home.

Madden had little time for Rutledge and considered his use of political correctness as *bloody tosh*. He favoured the old-style type of no-nonsense policing that his father, a former DCI, had so often expounded to him in his youth.

'This is it,' said Madden breaking the car. They got out and looked up at the grim concrete building, a product of the sixties building boom in London.

'He's on the second floor,' said Rutledge, consulting his pocket book. They entered the building and took the lift.

'What line are you going to take with this scumbag, guv?' said Madden as the lift came to a stop at the second floor.

'I'm not sure what you're getting at, Madden, and I object to being called "guv"—I consider "sir" to be a more fitting address for someone of my status. As to how

I'm going to deal with this *suspect*, I shall question him, and I want you to take meticulous notes of his answers.'

'Okey dokey, *sir*!' Madden replied and knocked loudly on Bottrell's door with a clenched fist.

Rutledge tutted audibly until the door was opened by Bottrell, wearing a dressing gown, with the bleary-eyed look of someone who just got out of bed.

Before he could speak, Rutledge presented his warrant card and said: 'I'm Detective Inspector Rutledge. This is Detective Constable Madden, and we should like to ask you a few questions. May we enter?'

'What's this all about? I work late at night and don't like being disturbed when I'm taking an afternoon nap.'

'We are most apologetic for disturbing your nap, sir, but we are investigating the suspicious death of a man named Reginald Meldrum, who, we understand, you know and—'

'Yes, I know all about that bastard. He was the man responsible for the death of my wife and daughter. I have to admit that I was very pleased to learn that he'd been found dead—suicide, wasn't it?'

'The matter is under investigation and it is necessary for us to eliminate certain people from our inquiries. You are one such person, so may—'

'All right, come in and ask your bloody questions and be quick about it!'

Bottrell led them into his sparsely furnished and untidy sitting room and sat down on a well-worn fireside chair. 'Right, inspector, fire away with your questions!'

'May we sit down?' Rutledge said.

'Yes, if you have to,' replied Bottrell, pointing to a tired looking settee.

They sat down and Rutledge took out his pocket book. 'You are Gary Bottrell of this address?'

'Yes, of course I am!'

Madden gave a heavy sigh and produced a dog-eared notebook and a biro.

'Where were you between the hours of 7 p.m. and midnight on Thursday last?'

Bottrell rubbed his unshaven jaw and pretended to think. 'Thursday evening, oh yes, I was at the theatre.'

'What theatre?' Rutledge said.

'Er… the Haymarket Theatre,' replied Bottrell.

'Is there anyone who can verify that you were there?' Madden asked.

Rutledge gave Madden a baleful glare, wishing that he'd asked the question.

'Yes, my girlfriend was with me. She wouldn't miss a visit to the theatre.'

'Where is your partner?' Rutledge asked.

'She's in bed—where I ought to be right now!' Bottrell almost shouted.

The door to the bedroom suddenly opened and a tussle-haired blonde woman, aged about 30, wearing a knee length black silk dressing gown walked into the room. 'What's all the bloody noise about, Gary—are you guys having a party?'

'No, Rita, these men are detectives and they want to

know where we were last Thursday evening. Will you tell them?'

'We were at the Haymarket Theatre, watching a re-run of *Showboat*,' Rita said. She walked to the sideboard, opened the top drawer and pulled out the programme for the show. The tickets for the show were stapled to the cover.

Madden couldn't be sure, but he thought he recognized Rita as a prostitute who operated in the New Cross area and picked up her *punters*—as they were called—in the nightclub where Bottrell worked. 'What's your surname, Rita?' he asked.

'Petchnik,' she replied and handed the programme to Rutledge.

Rutledge took it, examined the ticket stubs and said to Rita, 'What time did you attend the theatre?'

'We went there at seven and had a couple of drinks in the bar before the show started at about eight,' interposed Bottrell.

'What time did you leave the theatre?' Rutledge said.

'About ten-thirty,' Bottrell replied.

'Did you come straight back here?'

'Yes, after we'd called in at a takeaway for a curry.'

'And you remained here for the rest of the night?'

'Yes, we did!'

'Just one final question, Mr Bottrell, were you seen by anyone at the theatre who might be able to confirm that you were there?'

Bottrell screwed up his face in thought. 'Yes, I had

few words with one of the usherettes. She directed us to the wrong seats. She was bloody rude to me when I said I'd report her to the manager. Is that it, then?'

'Yes, for now, but we may have to see you both again.' Bottrell led them to the door.

'Goodnight, Mr Bottrell,' Rutledge said, as he and Madden walked out onto the landing.

'Goodnight,' Bottrell replied and closed the door.

CHAPTER TWELVE

'Your PA said you wanted to see me, sir,' said Hawksworth, standing in the Chief Superintendent's open doorway.

'Yes, I do, Ron. Come in and update me on the progress being made with the Meldrum case.'

'Well, sir, the good news is that according to DI Rutledge, we can probably eliminate our prime suspect from our inquiries.'

Sharif sighed deeply. 'Now tell me what the bad news is?'

'Well, if Bottrell is in the clear, we've nobody else in the frame and no other leads to follow.'

'Why is Rutledge so sure that Bottrell is in the clear?'

'I have his report here, in which he states that Bottrell's alibi is unshakeable. He was attending a show in the Haymarket Theatre with his girlfriend during the time that Meldrum was killed.'

'Is his girlfriend the only witness to that fact?'

'No, as it happens he had an altercation with an usherette. Apparently, she guided them to the wrong seats. He claims that the woman was rude to him when he rebuked her for the mistake.'

'So that's what Rutledge calls an unshakeable alibi! Has the usherette been questioned and confirmed his statement? Is it at all possible that Bottrell could have left the theatre sometime during the performance and killed Meldrum?'

'Well… er… I suppose that is possible, but Rutledge seems so sure that Bottrell is not our man.'

'Forget what Rutledge says! I'm not convinced that Bottrell wasn't in some way responsible for the death of Meldrum. Send DS Loomis to question the usherette and check with the theatre management to see if anything untoward occurred during the performance, which would be remembered by anyone present at the time. Oh, yes, and has Meldrum's house been checked for foreign fingerprints. If it hasn't, see that it's done and get Bottrell in to have his prints taken.'

'Right, sir, I'll get on to it right away.'

'Good, see that you do, because the Commander Homicide and Serious Crime has developed a personal interest in this case. So pull out all the stops, Ron, and get back to me as soon as you've made the necessary checks.'

* * * * *

DS Loomis accompanied by DC Madden drove to the Haymarket Theatre and a receptionist took them to the manager's office.

'These gentlemen are detectives, Mr Bairstow, and they're here to make enquiries about last Thursday's evening performance.'

'Thank you Julie, you may return to your duties,' Bairstow said.

Loomis and Madden produced their warrant cards and Loomis introduced them both.

'Please sit down and tell me what you want to know. I'm rather busy at the moment, so I hope this won't take long.'

'No need to worry on that account, Mr Bairstow. We're very busy too, so we won't take up much of your time. What I'd like to know is did anything occur in the theatre last Thursday which interrupted the performance or the normal routine?'

Bairstow looked a little puzzled. 'I'm not too sure what you want to know, Sergeant.'

'Well, did anyone create a disturbance during the show? Was there any need for the call: Is *there a doctor in the house?* Or did the curtains fail to open or close when required?'

'Oh, I see what you're getting at. Yes, in fact one of the cast members became ill just before the beginning of the last act and an understudy had to replace him. The director apologised to the audience after the final curtain.'

'Can you tell me at what time this occurred?' Loomis said.

'Yes, it would have been at about ten o'clock.'

'What time did the show end?'

'It was scheduled to finish at ten-thirty, but because of the slight delay with the recasting, it didn't finish until the director had addressed the audience at about ten-forty.'

DC Madden made a note of this in his pocket book.

'Just one other matter, did you receive any complaints from any of your patrons about an usherette being rude to them?'

'No, but I did receive a complaint from one of my usherettes that a patron had been rude to her. She said that the couple involved went to the wrong seats and when she tried to direct them to the right seats, the man blamed her for the mistake. He was most aggressive and said that he would report her to me. He never did. I put his unreasonable behaviour down to the fact that he might have had too many drinks in the bar before the show started.'

Loomis nodded. 'Yes, that's probably the answer. And that's all we need from you, sir. You've been most helpful and I don't think we'll need to see you again.'

Bairstow stood up. 'I'll see you out then.'

Loomis shook his head. 'No need for that, sir, we'll find our way okay. Goodbye.'

'Goodbye,' replied Bairstow and sat down at his desk to continue with what he had been doing before he was interrupted.

Driving back to their station with Madden at the wheel, Loomis expressed his satisfaction about the interview. 'All we need to do now is to get the SOCO team to check Meldrum's house for fingerprints other than his and then get Bottrell to come to the station to have his dabs taken.'

'So you're satisfied that Bottrell's not the man we

want, Sarge?' said Madden without taking his eyes of the road.

'Well, aren't you, Joe?'

'No, not entirely. I've got a hunch that this guy is a lot smarter then we think and has, somehow, pulled off a perfect crime.'

'Absolute nonsense, Joe! The problem with your thinking is that you treat every case like an Agatha Christie murder mystery. Focus on the facts, *Poirot*— Bottrell may be a bit of a shifty character, but I don't think he's a killer.'

Madden gave a slight shrug. 'Then all I've got to say to that is if he didn't kill Meldrum, then we've got a helluva case on our hands!'

'Okay, that's enough, Joe, just get us back to the station in quick time so that I can get my report to the DCI before I knock off for the night.'

CHAPTER THIRTEEN

'Well, did Loomis come up with anything new, Ron?' Sharif said as he glanced through Hawksworth's case file on the Meldrum investigation.

'He covered all the points we asked for. It's all in his report on the file.'

'I'm sure it is, Ron, but to save time, indulge me and enumerate his actions,' Sharif said with a rare smile as he handed the file back to Hawksworth.

'He interviewed the theatre manager, who told him that one of the usherettes had reported to him that a patron had been rude to her and threatened to report her to him, which he never did.'

'Before you continue, Ron, tell me if that suggests anything to you?'

'I'd say that it is quite likely that Bottrell realized his mistake in rebuking the usherette, for what was his mistake. Or, he didn't want to be bothered to report the matter to the manager.'

'Yes, I can see that answer would suit Loomis and Rutledge, but might Bottrell's motive for causing the need for the *rude exchanges* with the usherette been simply to provide him with a witness that he had attended the theatre at the same time as the murder was thought to have been committed?'

Hawksworth gave a pained look. 'Yes, sir, that is a possibility, but SOCO took Bottrell's fingerprints and found that he had not come to the notice of the police. They checked Meldrum's house and found no fingerprints other than those of Meldrum.'

Sharif gave a short laugh. 'Come, come, Detective Chief Inspector, if Bottrell, or anyone else had come to Meldrum's house with the planned intention to kill him they would, of course, have taken gloves along with the clothesline they used to hang him. As to the fact that he was said not to have any previous offences—so what! Few of the most notorious killers ever came to the notice of the police until they were arrested for murder!'

Hawksworth sighed deeply. He felt mentally overpowered by his chief superintendent's logical appraisal of the facts supplied by Loomis and made no comment.

'Well, Ron, carry on—what's next?'

Hawksworth consulted the file before he continued. 'The manager of the theatre said that one of the cast members had become ill and had to be replaced by his understudy before the final act. This and the director's apology to the audience caused a delay in the time that the show finally ended. This ties in with the time Bottrell said they left the theatre.'

'Hmm... so you're suggesting that Bottrell and his

companion were present when the recasting was done and when the director made his apology?'

'Yes, sir, everything points to that!'

'Did Loomis check with Bottrell to ascertain if he had been in the theatre when the curtain finally came down?'

Hawksworth riffled through the papers in the file before he answered. 'Loomis has made no mention of the fact, but I feel sure he will have done so.'

Sharif banged the desk with his fist. 'That is not good enough, Ron! That fact should have been in the report. It's vital evidence of Bottrell's presence when the show ended!'

'Right, sir, I'll send Loomis back to interview Bottrell again.'

'No, don't bother with that now, it's too late anyway. The weekend papers that review and report on shows will have made mention of the recasting because of the illness of the player. Therefore, we can never be sure that Bottrell was actually there, or that he read about the incident in the newspapers.'

'I must apologise for the apparent shortcomings in the investigation, sir.'

Sharif did not reply immediately, but looked steadily at Hawksworth who was wriggling uncomfortably in his chair. 'Now, I fully realize that you've only a few months to go before retirement and are no doubt looking forward to a quiet life, fishing in the River Thames at Sutton Courtney. However, until that time comes, you are a senior detective in my borough, so what I want you to do is to personally take charge of this investigation and, when necessary, do a bit of old-fashioned arse kicking to motivate your subordinates to greater efforts. Do I make myself clear, Ronald?'

Hawksworth's face flushed and his stomach churned. 'Yes, sir, you certainly do!'

'Then off you go and make sure I don't get any more half-baked reports from your troops!'

CHAPTER FOURTEEN

Larry and Louise Howard were watching a late night television film.

'What's it been like for you getting back to school?' Larry said in a too frequent commercial break.

'Just fine, Larry, I'm very pleased to be to back, teaching again. It gets my thinking back to normal. The head teacher and all my colleagues have been so supportive. It was also very gratifying to learn that my pupils said they had missed me.'

'I'm glad to hear that, but don't try to overdo it. You're far from being your old self yet.'

'Don't worry, I feel well on the way of making a complete recovery, but I do appreciate your concern. You would make a good husband and father, Larry. I'm surprised you've not found someone to share your life.'

'Well, I never met anyone while I was in the army and, anyway, I've got you to look after, until some lucky fellow comes along to sweep you off your feet!'

Louise gave a girlish laugh. 'We'll just have to wait and see about that. I'm quite happy as I am at the moment, thank you.'

The film ended and Larry switched over to a late night

news channel. A news reporter was interviewing a detective chief inspector who said that investigations were continuing into the violent deaths of two general building workers, who were referred to as cowboy builders, by people who were known to have employed them.

'From what I've read about the case, Larry, those two men seem quite similar. Both, because of their incompetence, were responsible for causing deaths. I know it's immoral to have such thoughts, but when I think of our parents being killed in the way they were, I can't find it in my heart to forgive that man Capstick. I'm sure that had he lived to face trial, he'd not have received much more than a couple of year's imprisonment.'

'You surprise me, Louise; I'd never have thought that you were against forgiveness, even for the most heinous crime. But of course, when one's parents are the victims, it's a different matter to the death of an unknown child.'

'Oh no, it isn't for me. I feel just as upset by the death of that mother and her child, caused by that man they found hanged. If he committed suicide, it might be his way of showing his remorse for what he'd done. If it was murder, I feel sorry that someone has taken the law into his own hands by killing him.'

'So what you are saying, Louise, is that you are totally against capital punishment and can never accept it, whatever the circumstances?'

'Yes, those are the principles I firmly hold and feel contempt for those low-life oiks one hears in public bars, propounding the return of capital punishment.'

'Good for you, Louise. If you feel you're right, hang onto your principles. I just hope that they'll never create an insuperable problem for you. Anyway, that's enough philosophizing for one evening. I don't know about you but I'm ready for bed,' Larry said as he picked up the newspaper and started to leave the room.

'Me too, Larry,' Louise said and switched off the television and lights and followed him up the stairs.

In bed Larry partook of a large brandy from his bedside locker—his usual nightcap, which he avoided drinking when Louise was present because her limit was an occasional glass of red wine and she was forever warning him about the dangers of exceeding the recommended number of alcoholic units.

He opened the newspaper to a report that he had noticed when quickly scanning the paper when it arrived. The report dealt with the assault and robbery of Arnold Prendergast, 82, a retired dentist, who lived alone in a large detached house near Shrewsbury Park. Two men later identified as Wayne Parfait, 25, and Jason Muscroft, 23, had called on Mr Prendergast and offered to repair his roof. They had seen that a single tile had slipped out of place and they told Prendergast that it would mean stripping off and replacing several rows of tiles to correct the fault. They said that the job would cost about two thousand pounds. Mr Prendergast refused to accept their offer and told them to leave. They then beat him unconscious with metal rods and stole money and items of jewellery from the house.

Apprehended, charged with causing grievous bodily harm and theft, the two men were remanded to appear at Woolwich Crown Court in six weeks and released on bail.

Mr Prendergast, who suffered extensive injuries to his head and limbs from the assault, was in intensive care at a local hospital.

Since the death of his parents and the reluctant agreement he had made with Bottrell, to take revenge against those responsible, he had researched the internet for similar cases. He found numerous reported cases of cowboy builders, who through incompetence, or sheer thoughtlessness, had been responsible for the death and injury of their clients. There were also cases where they had made exorbitant claims for the work they had done.

The more Howard read of past cases and the too lenient punishments given to those irresponsible and downright criminal activities of the cowboy builders, the angrier he became. To curb the unlawful and often quite dangerous activities of the so-called cowboy builders, he felt something needed to be done, but by whom? He then decided—I shall take on the task and mount a crusade against these evil men! I have nothing to lose. I have already killed and now feel no remorse for my act.

Howard finished his brandy and before falling into a deep sleep his final thought was his intention to enlist the aid and complicity of Gary Bottrell in his plans.

CHAPTER FIFTEEN

Howard got up at 6 a.m. and left a note for Louise, telling her he had to leave early for work because he had an early inspection to carry out.

He drove to Blackheath station and rang Bottrell from one of the public telephones. A full minute passed before Bottrell answered with a sleepy voiced: 'Hello, who's that ringing at this time of the morning?'

'It's me, Gary.'

'Why the hell are you ringing me at this time? I thought we had nothing more to say about anything!'

'Gary, just shut up and listen carefully to what I have to say.'

'Okay, but make it snappy because I had a late night at the club and planned to sleep until midday!'

'Never mind that, I want you to meet me in the *Duke of York* at 12 o'clock.'

'What the bloody hell for?'

'Just be there and you'll find out. If you're not there you can expect a call from the police to question you about the recording I made of our arrangement.'

'What are you—'

Howard replaced the phone, went back to his car and drove to his office.

* * * * *

At 11.50 in the morning, Howard entered the *Duke of York* and ordered a coffee and a ham sandwich.

Ten minutes later Bottrell came in and joined him at his table. 'What's this all about, Larry?'

'Get yourself a drink and I'll explain.'

Bottrell went to the bar and brought back a double whisky. He gulped down half of the drink with a loud slurp and said, 'Now what's this all about?'

'It's simply this, Gary. I've decided to wage war upon cowboy builders and I'm recruiting you to help me.'

Bottrell emptied his glass before he answered. 'You must be stark raving bonkers, if you think I'm sticking my neck out to help you in a crazy scheme like that!'

'No, Gary, I'm not mad and you're in no position to refuse to do what I ask of you.'

'You mean that you would give that bloody tape to the police? If you did you'd be up shit creek with me!'

'No, Gary, that's where you're wrong. The tape doesn't contain anything to incriminate me. In any case, I'm quite prepared to face the music if I'm caught. We've both committed, what we considered, justifiable killing of those responsible for causing the deaths of our families. I now want to carry on doing the same for other victims of cowboy builders.'

'Okay, you've got me by my short and curlies! What's in it for me, if I go along with this mad-brain scheme?'

Howard gave a short laugh. 'Financially—you'll receive absolutely nothing! But you will be doing a public service by ridding the area of some very nasty, money-grabbing exploiters of the most vulnerable—the aged and the unwary.'

'You have to be crazy, Larry, to think that I'd be willing to help you with what you're planning to do! But I'll make a deal with you. I'll help you on one occasion if you give me that blasted tape.'

'All right, you're on, Gary.' Howard pulled a newspaper cutting from his top pocket and handed it to Bottrell. 'Take this home with you and read it. The two guys we're after are Messrs Wayne Parfait and Jason Muscroft. They've been remanded to appear at the Woolwich Crown Court in about six weeks. I'll get back to you when I've found out where they live. We'll then plan our next move. Cheerio for now, Gary.'

Bottrell got up and without a word slouched out of the bar.

* * * * *

That evening Howard told Louise that he had some office paperwork to clear up and went to his room, where he kept his personal computer. He logged onto a website that could provide the addresses of persons registered on electoral rolls. He had no success in obtaining the address of Wayne Parfait, but he was able to obtain Jason Muscroft's address.

Early next morning Howard woke Bottrell up with a telephone call from Blackheath railway station. Before Bottrell could protest about the call, Howard said, 'I've got the address of one of them, so, with a little persuasion we should be able to get the address of his mate from him. Be at the *Duke of York* at midday.'

When Howard arrived at the *Duke of York* he was surprised to see that Bottrell was already there, seated at a table with a glass of whisky in front of him. Howard didn't bother getting a drink and a sandwich; he decided to have those later when he'd finished with Bottrell. 'I'm pleased to see that you're on parade early, Gary. How many whiskies have you had since you arrived?' Howard said with a grin.

'Don't try to patronise me; get on with what you've got to tell me! I want to get this job over and done with.'

'Be patient, this is going to take some careful planning and if you want to stay out of the hands of the police you're to follow my instructions. Firstly, here is Jason Muscroft's address.' Howard handed a slip of paper to Bottrell. 'Memorise it, then destroy it.'

Bottrell took the paper and glanced at it. 'I know Broadacre Gardens, Deptford, it's a right crappy block of flats; quite near where I live.'

'Good, that could make things easier for us. Muscroft lives in Flat 36, which is on the third floor. Tell me, Gary, does the front of the building face a main road?'

'Yes, the main road runs along the front of the building.'

'What about the bedrooms—are they situated at the back of the building?'

'Yes, they face a derelict factory. And a right bloody mess it is at the back of the flats.'

'Just what I was hoping for, Gary—the situation couldn't be better for our purpose.'

'What is our purpose?'

'I'll let you know about that when the time is right. For now, I just want you to make up some sort of disguise to alter your appearance. Make yourself look older. Don't wear a smart lounge suit. Dress like those who live at Broadacre Gardens. Buy second-hand clothes that you can destroy after the operation. Wear surgical gloves underneath leather gloves. Wear plain-soled shoes, or plimsolls. Do you get my drift, Gary?'

'Yes, bloody loud and clear, Sergeant Major! Just one thing though, when is this all going to take place?'

'Next Sunday, on your night off, we'll set off from here at 2200 hours and use your car, so pinch some plates to put over yours. We don't want to risk anyone seeing your vehicle's registered number when we're at the flats. The police always ask people living near a crime scene if they remember seeing any strange vehicles in the area.'

'Bloody hell, Larry, you're making this sound like some sort of military operation behind enemy lines!'

'Yes, Gary, that's what it is and there's nothing wrong with using a bit of military planning. It paid off for Monty at El Alamein and the landings at Normandy on D-Day!'

'Can I be dismissed now, General?' Bottrell said with deliberate sarcasm.

'Yes, but don't forget what I've told you and be parked a few yards up the road from the *Duke of York* at 2155 hours on Sunday!'

Bottrell gave Howard a mock salute and marched out of the pub.

* * * * *

At about 10 p.m. that evening Howard, dressed in his disguise, drove to Broadacre Gardens to do what he would call a recce of the building. It was, as Bottrell had described, a run-down block of flats, poorly lit, with all manner of rubbish tipped at the back of the building. He located Flat 36 and saw that there was a light in the living room and the kitchen.

A perfect venue for what he had in mind, Howard thought as he drove home.

CHAPTER SIXTEEN

DCI Hawksworth called a full-scale meeting of all the detectives engaged in the Meldrum and Capstick cases. DI Rutledge, DS Loomis and about a dozen other detectives were present.

Hawksworth stood behind a rostrum with two fat crime case files in front of him. 'Right, now listen up. The Chief Superintendent is very unhappy over the progress we're making with the Meldrum and Capstick cases. The top brass are on his back and he wants a maximum effort to solve these two cases of murder. Yes, it's now been established that both men were murdered. You are all aware of the facts behind these cases and what I want you to do is to put some fresh thinking into the motives and any possible link between the two cases. DI Rutledge, will you start us off by putting your point of view forward for general consideration?'

Rutledge rose, straightened his tie and cleared his throat before he spoke. 'Yes, boss. As you are aware, I have submitted two very concise reports into the circumstances of the deaths of these two men. I am sure that we are dealing with two different killers, both of whom carefully planned and violently executed the murders of Capstick and Meldrum. Both victims were casual odd-job men or so-called cowboy builders. Both had been responsible for the deaths of several people through neglect and incompetence and were awaiting trial. My initial belief was that relatives of their victims were responsible for taking revenge on them. However, after examining all the evidence and interviewing the two suspects, I'm firmly of the opinion that that they had not been involved in any way.'

'Thank you, Bob. Now if any of you wish to add anything to what DI Rutledge has said, now's your opportunity.'

DS Loomis stood up. 'Yes, sir, I'd like to add my endorsement to what DI Rutledge has expressed.'

'That's all very well, Sergeant, but if our original suspects are in the clear, who are we looking for and what possible motive could they have?'

Loomis looked at Rutledge, as if to say, 'What's the answer to that, guv?' But Rutledge sat tight-lipped and ignored him.

Loomis shuffled his feet and looked uncomfortable before he continued. 'Well, they could have had differences with others of similar ilk. Like squabbling over jobs they'd been contracted to do, or perhaps they had personal reasons… but no doubt motives will come to light when we arrest the killers.'

Hawksworth, wearing a pained look, spread his arms and shook his head. 'Coincidence, coincidence, too many coincidences, and coincidences don't often occur in murder investigations. There are too many killers with the same motive—revenge, and, as far as has been ascertained, the two victims had no connection with each other save the way they made their living.' Hawksworth looked around the assembly. 'Has anybody else got a theory? If you have, let's hear it.'

DC Madden got slowly to his feet. 'I may be sticking my neck out here and might live to regret it, but apart from the fact that we know that Capstick and Meldrum were murdered, I don't agree with anything that has been said. I'm of the opinion that they were revenge killings and that the two obvious suspects were personally involved in the killings, or they hired a hit man to do the job for them. This links the murders and to prove my theory I feel that we should be spending time looking into the backgrounds of Bottrell and Howard who have another link; they both served in the Army.'

Rutledge and Loomis glowered at Madden as he sat down.

Hawksworth looked intently at Madden before he spoke. 'I can't say that I'm in complete agreement with what you say, but you've opened up a possible fresh line of inquiry. So, go to it, Madden, and spend some time looking into the backgrounds of these two *possible* suspects and report back to me directly with whatever you find out. As for the rest of you, I want you to go through all the evidence to hand and delve deeper into the previous jobs carried out by Capstick and Meldrum, to see if you can ferret out any of their customers who may have had good reason to have killed them.'

CHAPTER SEVENTEEN

At 9.45 on Sunday evening, Howard waited outside the *Duke of York* for the arrival of Bottrell. It was a wet and windy evening, which pleased Howard, because the bad weather would mean fewer people out on the streets. He had driven to Broadacre Gardens earlier in the evening and spotted Muscroft moving about in his kitchen.

Bottrell pulled up near the pub and Howard quickly got in the car. Howard gave him a once over, noting that he was wearing heavy framed spectacles, a moustache and a beard. He was dressed in a shabby overcoat and wearing a misshapen slouch hat that covered most of his light brown hair.

'Yes, you've got a good disguise, Gary, you're hardly recognisable. Before we take off, there's just a few checks I want to make. Are you wearing surgical gloves under those leather gloves, and are those smooth-soled shoes?'

'Yes, and before you ask, I've changed the number plates on the car!'

'That's very good. Have you been drinking this evening?'

'No, I haven't, but I could do with a drink right now!'

'You can drink all you want once we've done what we're going to do. Now take us to Broadacre Gardens.'

Bottrell put the car into gear and drove off.

'Well, what's the drill when we get to Muscroft's flat, Larry?'

'We knock on his door and invite ourselves in and ask him to ring his pal, Wayne, and invite him to come to his flat.'

'Just like that, eh?'

'Yes, Gary, just like that, and there's no need for you to know any more at this stage, so just keep within the speed limit.'

The rain was easing off and the wind had dropped when they arrived at the flats. Howard told Bottrell to drive around to the back of the flats and park the car.

Howard and Bottrell walked around to the front of the building and Howard looked up at Flat 36. The light was still on in the kitchen and Muscroft's shape was visible through net curtains. They quietly climbed the two flights of stairs to the third floor and walked along the passageway to Flat 36. Howard rapped on the front door. A few seconds later Muscroft opened the door. Before he could utter a word Howard hit him on the side of the neck and caught him in his arms before he fell to the floor.

'Shut the door and help me lift him into the sitting room,' ordered Howard.

They carried the unconscious Muscroft into the sitting room and placed him on a sofa.

'He's not dead, is he?' Bottrell said.

Howard laughed. 'No, not yet. I didn't hit him hard enough to do any permanent damage.'

'What was that you used, Judo?'

'Yes, something like that. Go into the kitchen and get me a saucepan of cold water.'

Bottrell returned with a jug of water. 'I couldn't find a saucepan.'

Howard took the jug and emptied the water over Muscroft's head.

Muscroft moaned and he opened his eyes. 'What the fuck are you doing to me?'

'We just want you to phone Wayne and tell him that you want to see him about a good two-man job that should make a lot of money. You want to give him all the details tonight so that you can see the punter tomorrow to line up the job. Now here's a piece of paper with that message written on it!'

Muscroft tried to get up, but Howard pushed him back onto the sofa.

'Where's your phone, Jason?'

'My mobile's in my jacket. It's hanging on the hallstand. Why are you doing this to me?' Muscroft said, pleadingly.

Howard ignored him. 'Fetch his phone, Gary.'

Gary returned with the jacket and took the phone from an inside pocket.

Howard took it and passed it to Muscroft. 'Now phone Wayne.'

Muscroft was visibly quaking with fear. 'Why do I have to do that?'

Howard grabbed Muscroft's ear and twisted it. 'Because if you don't I'll pull your ears off!'

Still shaking, Muscroft dialled a number. Howard thrust the piece of paper in front of his face. 'When he answers, read this message to him. If you try to say anything else I'll break your arms.'

Parfait answered the phone and Muscroft read the message, haltingly.

Parfait must have queried the message, because Muscroft answered, 'It's important that you come tonight, Wayne.' Howard snatched the phone from Muscroft and switched it off.

Howard pulled a length of clothesline from under his raincoat and handed it to Bottrell.

'Make a noose at one end of this and securely tie the other end around the leg of the bed in the bedroom. Then push the bed up to the window.'

Bottrell looked puzzled but didn't question Howard's instructions and returned to the sitting room a few minutes later. 'Okay, I've done what you wanted; now tell me what happens next.'

'I'm hoping that the next thing to happen is that Wayne joins us,' Howard said with a brief smile.

'And what happens when Wayne arrives?' Bottrell said.

Howard grinned broadly. 'We're going to have a party.'

'A party—what sort of party?'

'It's going to be a Wild West party for cowboys who've broken the law.'

Bottrell shook his head. 'Are you losing your marbles, Larry?'

'No, everything will become clear when Wayne arrives. Now, until he does will you make another noose with this rope as before and tie it to another leg of the bed?'

'Oh, I begin to see what's going to happen.'

'Now, Gary, remember the old army saying: *No names no pack drill* or *Mum's the word* or something like that.'

Gary nodded sagely and took the rope into the bedroom.

There was a knock at the door. Howard waited until Bottrell returned to the sitting room to watch Muscroft while he opened the door to Wayne.

'Come in and join the party, Wayne, we've been expecting you.'

'Who the fuck are you, old man? I've come to see my mate, Jason.'

'Come in then, Wayne, he's in the sitting room,' Howard said letting him lead the way and then putting a head lock on him and dragging him into the sitting room and throwing him on the floor and placing his foot on his throat. 'I think the party is complete now, Gary,' Howard said as he dragged Wayne off the floor and pushed him onto the sofa with Jason.

'What the fuck's going on, Jason? I thought you got me here to talk about a job.'

Jason croaked and rubbed his throat.

'Shut up the pair of you!' roared, Howard. 'What we'd

like to know is what have you two got to say for yourselves for beating up Mr Arnold Prendergast, an 82-year-old man, so badly injured that he is in hospital and near death? You did that all because he wouldn't let you cheat him. Then, after leaving him unconscious, you stole his money and jewellery, including his wedding ring, which you ripped off his finger.'

Wayne pulled himself off the recumbent Jason. 'You can't treat us like this; you're too bloody old to be bleedin' coppers.'

Howard gave a short low laugh. 'No, unfortunately for you, we're not coppers! We seek only justice for Mr Prendergast. So, if you've nothing to say in your defence we'll get on with the party.'

Jason pushed himself free of Wayne and cried out, 'What party? All you've done is hit me and pushed us around.'

Howard produced a blackjack (a souvenir of his time with a US Army unit) from his raincoat pocket and slapped Jason on the side of the head. Jason fell forward off the sofa. 'Take him into the bedroom and prepare him for the necktie party, Gary.'

Gary grabbed Jason's arms and dragged him into the bedroom.

Wayne had seen enough western films to know what a necktie party was and hurled himself at Howard, who sidestepped and hit him with the blackjack. He crumpled up on the floor. Howard lifted him up and dragged him into the bedroom. Bottrell was putting the noose over

Jason's head and pulling it tight. Howard dropped Wayne on the bed and opened the window. 'You can let that one go now, Gary, while I get this cowboy ready to join him.'

Bottrell pushed Wayne through the open window. There was a cracking noise as Wayne fell the length of the rope, causing the bed to bang against the wall. Howard finished putting the noose around Jason's neck and pushed him over the window ledge. He collided with the hanging Wayne and ended up alongside him, swinging against the bedroom window on the floor below.

'Time for us to mosey along, pardner,' Howard said, in imitation of Gary Cooper acting in a western film.

'You're right there, Larry! If anyone's in that bedroom below they'll be investigating the banging against their window.'

Howard and Bottrell hurried out of the flat, shutting the door as they went. They got into the car and Bottrell drove away quietly.

The residents in the flat below number 36 weren't in their bedroom, but were in the sitting room watching, ironically, a western film, featuring a long-drawn out gunfight.

However, there were witnesses, a teenaged boy and girl, who were snogging against the wall of the derelict factory. Tracey pushed Alfie away and looked up at the flats. 'Alfie, it looks as though there's two men hanging out of the window of one of the flats!'

Alfie spun around and looked across at the building. 'Yes, you're right Tracey. Let's get a closer look.'

They walked across the waste ground to the block and stood under the two hanging figures. 'They're not moving, they must be dead!' Alfie exclaimed excitedly. 'I'll ring the police on my mobile.'

'How awful! I don't think we should hang around here,' said Tracey, clutching Alfie's arm.

'No, we'll go as soon as I've rung 999.' Alfie dialled the number, which was answered immediately. 'What service do you want?'

'The police, because there's two men hanging out of a third floor bedroom window at Broadacre Gardens, in Deptford and I think they're dead!' Alfie said in a faltering voice.

'The police control room operator said, 'Stay just where you are and officers will be sent to investigate your report.'

* * * * *

Bottrell stopped his car around the corner of the *Duke of York*, where Howard had parked his car.

'Well, that operation went rather well, don't you think, Gary?'

'Oh, yes, I haven't had such fun for ages. It's a pity they don't hang murderers any more. If they did, I'd apply for the job.'

Howard laughed as he got out of the car. 'I really think you're serious, Gary. I'll be in touch sometime. Goodnight.'

Bottrell leaned out of the car. 'Hey, you've forgotten something, haven't you? Where's that damned tape?'

'Oh, yes, the tape. You didn't expect me to carry it about with me, did you? It's in a safety deposit box at my bank. I'll retrieve it as soon as I can get around to it.'

Bottrell's face took on a look of rage. 'You'd better make that soon, or you'll find out how angry I get if I'm crossed!'

'I'll keep that in mind, Gary—goodnight!' Howard turned away and walked to his car. Inside he took off his disguise, bagged it and tossed it on the back seat. He'd put it in the boot when he got home. He looked at his watch, it was 11.15. Louise was probably in bed asleep or watching her television. She'd want to know where he'd been so late. He thought he'd tell her that he'd attended a reunion of his old army comrades. That would sound reasonable to her.

CHAPTER EIGHTEEN

Chief Superintendent Sharif was on leave, so DCI Hawksworth was briefing the deputy Borough commander, Superintendent Lauren Armitage, about the two dead men found hanging out of a bedroom window the previous night.

The superintendent, although only in her early thirties, was a high-flying officer destined to reach chief officer rank at an early age. She was tall, physically attractive and had a commanding presence. She had a sense of humour, but was not one to suffer fools or those who attempted to seek her favour by being overly acquiescent.

'So, what's the score on this one, Ron?'

Hawksworth delved into his briefcase and pulled out a sheaf of papers. 'I've got the pathologist's preliminary report, which states that both men died as a result of hanging. Their necks were broken, but the pathologist reported that both men had bruises on the side of their head, probably caused by a blunt weapon—possibly some sort of truncheon. We might learn a bit more about how they died when the autopsy has been carried out.'

'What do we know about this pair?'

'Well, ma'am, you will remember the Prendergast case; these were the two men who assaulted and robbed Mr Prendergast in his home. They were awaiting trial.'

'Yes, of course I remember he case; they were cowboy builders named Wayne Parfait and Jason Muscroft. By the way, what is the latest condition of their victim?'

'Sadly, the hospital notified us this morning that Mr Prendergast had died during the night. Ironically, at about the same time that Parfait and Muscroft had died.'

'It would seem that we have an extraordinary case on our hands. Four so-called cowboy builders murdered— three of them by hanging. Have you any idea what sort of killer or killers we're after?'

'I'm sure that there are at least two people involved in all the killings. I believe the motive for the killings is revenge for the deaths caused by these men. I have assigned DI Rutledge and his section to go over all the evidence we have so far and apply some fresh thinking to the case. The one exception to the thinking that none of the relatives of the victims is responsible for the murders is DC Madden. He firmly believes that Gary Bottrell and Laurence Howard are responsible for all the killings and are conducting a sort of vendetta against cowboy builders. I detailed him to prove his theory by delving into the backgrounds of Bottrell and Howard.'

'So, you're hedging your bets on this one, Ron? You're half thinking that Madden may have the right idea. From what you've told me and from what I've read about the case, I've come to the conclusion that we might be looking for some sort of self-appointed Judge Roy Bean, who was known in the late 19th century as the only "Law West of the Pecos" and who had an exaggerated reputation for hanging wayward cowboys.'

'You have the advantage of me there, ma'am, I'm not familiar with the history of that judge.'

'Don't give it a thought, Ron; I was just letting my imagination loose on you. But, seriously, if the relatives of those who were killed through the malpractice, carelessness, or incompetence of the cowboy builders, were not their killers, it might be that we are dealing with a vigilante group, bent on taking revenge on behalf of the their victims. I suggest you give Madden all the rope he needs—no pun intended—to follow his hunch.'

'Right, ma'am, I'll see to that. Is there anything else you wish to discuss?'

'No, not at the moment, Ron, but do keep me fully updated on any progress made. It would be a feather in all our caps if we could close the files on these murders before the chief gets back from leave.'

Walking back to his office, Hawksworth thought, I only wish we could close the file before Sharif gets back. Superintendent Armitage is much easier to deal with.

Later that day he called DI Rutledge, who had been in charge of the crime scene, to his office. 'Have SOCO thoroughly examined Muscroft's flat?'

'Yes, they certainly have, but apart from traces of water having been splashed on the back of the sofa, they found nothing to give us a clue as to who was present in the flat other than the two victims.'

'Oh, Bob, surely I don't need to remind you that the

perpetrators of any crime always leave something of themselves behind at the scene of their crime? This evidence is sometimes very difficult to find, but can be invaluable to the investigating officer.'

'Right guv, I'll get the SOCO team to give the place another going over.'

'Aside from looking for foreign DNA and bits of material from the killers' clothes, what about the rope that was used to hang Parfait and Muscroft? Has that been compared with the rope that was used to hang Meldrum?'

'Yes, of course, guv.'

'Then I suppose you've checked all of the shops that sell such rope to ascertain if any of their customers made a purchase of a fairly large quantity of the rope?'

'Guv, I only got that information from SOCO this morning that the rope was the same used for the three hangings, and I was just about to send a couple of DCs out to visit all the shops that sell rope, when you called me,' lied Rutledge'

'Well, see it's done straightaway. There can't be many shops that sell rope. Clotheslines are usually made of plastic these days.'

'Right, I'll get onto that straightaway. Is there anything else?'

'Yes, ask DC Madden to report to me as soon as he comes back from wherever he is.'

When Rutledge got back to the CID general office, he found DC Madden peering into the monitor of a computer.

'The DCI wants to see you, DC Madden. You'd better

drop what you're doing and see what he wants from you. I hope you've got some useful information that'll please him and you'd better mind your Ps and Qs, because he's not in a very good mood at the moment,' said Rutledge in pompous manner.

Madden didn't acknowledge the remark. He knew that it was Rutledge's pompous way of putting down those he considered his inferiors. He logged off the case, switched off the computer and walked out of the office without a word.

'DI Rutledge told me that you wanted to see me, sir.'

'Yes, Joe, I do. Come in, close the door, take a seat and tell me what you've found out about your fancied suspects.'

'In short, sir, plenty. Both of these men served in the Army, Howard in the REME and Bottrell in the RMP so I checked their Army record offices. They were most helpful and gave me the following information,' said Madden consulting his pocket book. 'Laurence Howard served 22 years as an electrical mechanical NCO and reached the rank of warrant officer 2nd class. He was described as having an exemplary character and served with distinction in Iraq and Afghanistan, where, after very limited training, he was employed neutralizing IEDs. He was mentioned in dispatches on two occasions for his dedication to duty, when under fire from Taliban insurgents. Since retiring from the army, he's been employed by the Greenwich Borough Council as a clerk of works. His employers speak highly of his work ethic and describe him as a man of irreproachable character.'

Madden paused for Hawksworth to digest what he had said.

'Hmm… he doesn't sound like a man who would commit murder,' said Hawksworth, stroking his unshaven chin. 'What have you found out about Bottrell?'

'He's about as different to Howard as he could be—like chalk and cheese. He served for about ten years as a corporal in the Royal Military Police. His record shows that he was charged with causing grievous bodily harm to a young private soldier, who was in his custody. For this, he was court martialled, stripped of his rank, sentenced to 56 days detention and dishonourably discharged from the army. His previous commanding officers described him as a foul-mouthed bully, who drank too much and was considered generally unfit for the role of a military policeman. Since his discharge from the army, five years ago, he's been employed as a door manager (what we would call a "bouncer") in the Top Spot Club, which is a seedy nightclub in New Cross. It specialises in gambling and providing evening hostesses (what we might call "prostitutes") for their clients. Bottrell has some sort of loose relationship with one of the girls named Rita Petchnik. I believe he used her to help alibi himself on the night of Meldrum's murder. When I asked the manager of the Top Spot Club, what he thought about Bottrell, all he said was that Bottrell was always smartly dressed and handled himself well. What he meant was that Bottrell never had any bother keeping undesirables out of the club. I had to smile at that, because the place is always full of undesirables! As to his personal life, he's separated from his wife and lives alone in a manky flat in Deptford, where he often entertains women he's picked up in the club. His only child, a daughter, died along with her mother from carbon monoxide fumes. I spoke to his former neighbours who said that he idolised his daughter and often came to see her, bringing expensive gifts.'

'You've certainly done a thorough job there, Joe. On the face of it Bottrell could be the killer of Steve Capstick, the man responsible for the death of his wife and daughter, but I don't think he's the sort man who'd risk his freedom by taking revenge on a cowboy builder, on behalf of someone else who had experienced a similar tragedy.'

'Shall I continue with my enquiries, sir? I still think that there's a link between these two men, and if there is I'll find it.'

'Yes, carry on as you've been doing. And I've a bit of good news for you. The Chief Superintendent supported my recommendation for you to be appointed acting detective sergeant while you are involved in this case. I know that you passed your sergeants' promotion examination about five years ago, so I feel sure that if you get this case cleared up your promotion to substantive sergeant will follow. I'll let DI Rutledge know that you are to be released from his section and will report directly to me.'

'Thank you, sir,' said Madden, as he rose to leave, 'I'm most grateful for your confidence in me and I'll do my utmost to get the result we all want.'

'I'm sure you will, Joe,' Hawksworth smiled.

CHAPTER NINETEEN

Howard was at Blackheath railway station telephoning Bottrell.

Bottrell answered in a sleepy voice. 'I don't have to guess who's ringing me at this time of the morning. What do you want now that's so important at this early hour, Larry?'

'Have you seen yesterday's local newspaper?'

'Yes, and I bet you've rung me to ask if I'd read all about that poor old bugger who was electrocuted in his kitchen, because someone had left an uncovered live wire behind his toaster?'

'Good, I'm glad you're keeping up with all the local news about the activities of cowboy builders. The man involved, if you've forgotten, is Darrell Potter, who, it's been reported, is an unqualified electrician. Apparently he'll take on any job if the money is right and he can con the unwary householder into believing he's fully qualified to do what they require.'

'I can almost hear your brain working overtime in planning a way to make another *cowboy* bite the dust!'

'You're showing a remarkable insight into my

thinking this morning, Gary. You seem to have a clearer head than usual. Are you on the wagon?'

'No, I'm bloody well not and every time you ring I open another bottle. So, for fuck's sake get to the point of your call. And while you're on, what about that damn tape?'

'You'll get your tape, I promise, but I want you to first help me with the disposal of Mr Potter.'

'What's it to be, another lynching?'

'No, I've decided to update the method of execution. It'll take the form of electrocution. Appropriate in this case, don't you think?'

'What do I have to do?'

'It might be a good idea for you to do a recce of the area where he lives. His address is 52 Bartholomew Road in Deptford. It's a two up and two down, terrace house. Fortunately, he lives alone, which will make the job easier. See if you can find out if he remains in during the evening. Make sure you're in your disguise, though.'

'If you want me to help it'll have to be on a Sunday or Monday night.'

'Okay, do your recce on Sunday evening and meet me around the corner at the end of his road, which leads to Haddon Road, at 22.00 hours on Monday night. Is that clear?'

'Yes, I'll be there. And don't you forget to bring that tape with you.'

'Never mind the tape! Just make sure you're there at 22.00 hours.'

'Supposing he's not at home at 22.00 hours—what do we do then?'

'If he's not there we'll break into his house and wait for him to return.'

* * * * *

'So, you're off out again tonight, Larry,' said Louise, while they were having their evening meal. 'I suppose you'll be meeting up with some of your old army pals.'

'Yes, that's what I had in mind. You're not bothered about being alone for a couple of hours, are you?'

'No, of course not, but I thought you would want to join me in watching that new crime series starting tonight.'

'What is it, another of those crime dramas, implausible, predictable and investigated by detectives with flawed characters, who solve their cases, despite spending so much time sorting out their own and their families' problems?'

Louise gave a brief laugh. 'So, crime dramas are losing your interest. What you need is a girlfriend to take out rather than meeting up with all those boozy old soldiers. Anyway, I had something I wanted to discuss with you tonight.'

'Oh yes, and what was that?'

'Never mind, it can wait until you've more time for conversation.'

Larry looked at his watch—seven-forty-five. 'I've

plenty of time. I shan't be going out until about nine, so tell me what's on your mind.'

Louise cheeks glowed and her eyes sparkled. 'What I have to tell you is that I have made friends with a man and was thinking about bringing him home one evening. That's of course, if you have no objection.'

'Is that all? Of course you can invite him here. This is your home now, so you don't need my permission to bring your friends home. They'll be good company for you when I go out with my *boozy old soldier friends.*'

'Lovely! I'll invite him here for Wednesday evening. I'll tell him to come at seven and after we've had a couple of drinks I'll phone for some takeaway meals. What do you think, Indian?'

'That's okay by me. Make it Indian. It should suit him. It's supposed to be the nation's favourite meal.'

'Hmm, I'm not sure he'd be happy with Indian curry. I know he favours Chinese food, as I do.'

'Oh, so you've known him long enough to be aware of his culinary tastes?'

'Well yes, he visits the school quite often and has lunch in our canteen.'

'What's his job, some sort of schools' inspector?'

Louise shook her head. 'Oh no, he's a policeman—PC Tony Jarvis, our school liaison officer.'

Larry gulped and took a deep breath. A police office visiting the house might prove to be a problem, he thought. He quickly gained his composure. 'Hmm… he might have something more interesting to talk about other than examination pass rates, student truancy and parent teacher meetings.'

'Yes, I'm sure you will have much in common with him. For a start he plays golf and chess and you're always saying that you don't know anyone to play with.'

'How old is he?'

'He was thirty-four last week.'

'Thirty-four and still a constable? He doesn't sound very ambitious.'

'You're quite wrong in believing that, because he's passed the examination for promotion to sergeant and hopes to be promoted within the next year. In the meantime, he's being transferred to the CID as an aide, a sort of probationary detective, as soon as a vacancy occurs. It was his choice to remain in his present job as a school liaison officer. He is successful in that role and we'll be sorry to lose him.'

'I shouldn't worry too much. I'm sure you'll get a suitable replacement. The care and mentoring of children is a top priority in these troubled times. Anyway, I look forward to meeting your constable on Wednesday evening. Now I must leave you to get ready for my evening with my boozy soldier friends.'

* * * * *

Howard, wearing his disguises, arrived at Haddon Road at 9.50 in the evening, to find that Bottrell was there, and parked in the side of the road, away from a streetlight. He took a small suitcase out of his car and went to Bottrell's car. Bottrell got out of his car and stood to attention on the pavement. 'I'm all present and correct, sir,' he said grinning inanely.

'Good! I'm glad to see you're correctly attired, Corporal,' answered Howard in a pompous tone as though he were a newly commissioned second lieutenant inspecting a squad of soldiers. 'Right, that's enough silly banter. Have you anything to report about Potter?'

'Yes, he's in. I drove slowly past his house; his van was parked outside; the lights were on in the sitting room and his television was on so loud that I could hear it outside.'

'Right, let's do what we came to do,' Howard said, leading the way to 52 Bartholomew Road. As they approached Potter's house Howard noted that there were no lights on in numbers 50 and 54. He pressed the doorbell three times before Potter came to the door.

'Yes, what do you want? If you're collecting for charity, you're unlucky, I don't—'

'No, Mr Potter, we're not collecting for charity; what we want is to engage you to do some electrical work in our house. Your name has been recommended to us by a friend.'

Potter smiled smugly and opened the door wider. 'Then you've come to the right man. I've not much on at the moment, so I can fit you in straightaway. Come in and let me know what you want done.'

Potter led them into his untidy sitting room, which

exuded a smell of stale food and an unpleasant body odour. Potter turned off the television. He then invited them to sit down. 'So, what can I do for you gents?'

'First let me introduce ourselves,' said Howard, and continued: 'My name is Roger Plenderleith and this is my brother Arnold. What we want is some upgrading work done to our bathroom.'

'There's no problem with that for me. I specialise in modernising bathrooms and kitchens. I could come to your home tomorrow and we can see what wants doing. By the way, where do you live?'

'If you'll excuse me, talking about bathrooms has caused me to want to use your loo. I'm afraid I've got the old man's complaint—a rather weak bladder.'

'That's okay Mr Plenderleith—help yourself. The lavatory is in the bathroom on the landing.'

'Thank you. We can get down to business when I've relieved myself.'

Howard climbed the stairs and entered the bathroom. As he expected, it contained only a rather chipped and stained bath, a not very hygienic looking lavatory and a cracked sink, but apart from a plastic garden chair, no furniture. A grey-looking bath towel hung over the back of the chair. There was no form of heating in the room, nor was there anything in the room upon which a small electric fire might be placed. Looking around the walls, he saw a picture on the wall at the end of the bath of a naked woman stepping into a bath. He removed the picture. There was no picture hook, just a simple wire nail.

He tried to waggle the nail and found that it was firmly held in the wall. He took a tape measure from his pocket and measured the distance from the nail to the floor and then from under the door to a power point on the landing wall. He replaced the picture, flushed the toilet and returned to the sitting room.

When he entered, Bottrell and Potter were deep in conversation about the merits of London soccer teams.

'Can I get you chaps some refreshment—a beer, or a soft drink, if you're driving?'

'No thanks, Darrell,' said Howard. 'If you don't mind I'd like to get on with what we came here for, to talk about bathroom improvements and there's no better place to do that than in a bathroom.'

'I'm afraid my bathroom needs major refurbishment. With all the work I do for my customers I've not had the time to do anything for myself,' said Potter with a sheepish grin.

'Yes, I did notice that, but no matter, our bathroom is about the same size as yours so with the knowledge of what needs to be done in your bathroom can be applied to ours,' said Howard as he picked up the case he had brought into the house and placed at the side of his chair.

'Okay, the customer is always right, so let's get on with it,' said Potter, leading them up the stairs.

As they entered the bathroom, Howard struck Potter in the back of his neck. Potter fell to the floor unconscious.

'Gary, strip off all his clothes and place them neatly on that chair.'

Howard removed the picture from the wall. Next, he took an electric fire and an extension cable from the case. He hooked the wire handle of the fire over the nail and inserted the cable's plug into the socket on the landing.

Bottrell didn't need to be told what to do next. He put the bath plug in and turned on both taps. When the bath was half-full he turned the taps off and Howard helped him lift Potter from the floor and placed him into the bath.

Potter came to and thrashed around in the bath. 'What the fuck's going on!'

Bottrell pushed Potter down into the bath and held him down with a hand over his head.

'Keep still, Potter, and listen to what I have to say. There's an old man called Arnold Haydon who's lying, near dead, in a hospital bed. And it's because of your shoddy and incompetent workmanship that he's there. Have you anything to say in your defence?'

Potter tried desperately to free himself from Bottrell's hold on his head. Bottrell pushed his head under the water and Potter came up spluttering.

'It was an accident! It's not my fault the old fool was electrocuted. I was called away to another job. He must have been a bloody idiot to grab hold of a live wire. Let me go!' he shouted in a quavering voice.

'No, I'm sorry but I cannot let you go, because if I do you will continue to call yourself an electrician and carry out incompetent work that could cause death or injury to your unwary customers, or should I say victims!'

Potter looked up at the electric fire and it began to

dawn on him what these two old men were planning to do to him. He splashed the water with his arms and sobbed. 'Please let me go, I swear I'll never do another job as an electrician.'

Bottrell looked knowingly at Howard who nodded. Bottrell let go of Potter's head as Howard unhooked the electric fire from the wall and hurled it into the bath. There was a tremendous flash, a gut-wrenching scream from Potter and a bang as the fuse was blown.

'Check his life-signs Gary. It's safe to touch him now the fuse has blown,' Howard said as he wrenched at the nail that had held the electric fire. As he slowly eased the nail out he dragged it downward to give the effect that the weight of the fire had dislodged it. He dropped the nail into the bath.

'He's deader than a grilled kipper!' said Bottrell with a mirthless laugh.

'Then we can say that it's been a job well-executed, Gary. Now all we've got to do is to check that we've left nothing behind that'll provide the police with a clue to us having been here.'

'I don't think that's likely. We've worn gloves all the time.'

'Yes, but as an ex-military copper, you should know that fingerprints aren't the only evidence the police look for. They spend a lot of time searching for DNA samples. They claim that an intruder always leaves something behind. Had we had a drink, smoked a cigarette, taken our caps off, shed some hair, left some blood or other bodily fluids, they'd have found what they were looking for and should either of us have been arrested at some time they would have taken a sample of our DNA for comparison with that found at the crime scene.'

'Bloody hell, Larry, you do go on! We ought to be getting out of here. What are you going to do with that picture?'

'Well, we can't hang it back on the wall, because we want the police to think that the fire was always there.'

'I'll take it then. It'll look good in my bathroom,' Bottrell said with a leer.

Howard led the way back to the sitting room, calling over his shoulder, 'Leave the bathroom light on. The lighting circuit hasn't been blown.'

They both checked the chairs where they had been sitting, and left all the downstairs lights on. Potter wouldn't have turned them off when he went for a bath.

Howard quietly opened the front door and looked out on the deserted street. They went out, Howard with his empty suitcase and Bottrell with the picture tucked under his arm. Howard quietly shut the door. They walked back, in silence, to where their cars were parked.

'Well, where's the tape?'

'Oh, yes, the tape, Gary,' said Howard, withdrawing a slim cassette from his overcoat pocket and passing it to Bottrell, 'and you can have this case to carry your picture in.'

'So ends our *beautiful friendship*,' said Bottrell with a sneer. He put the cassette in his overcoat pocket and put the picture in the case before getting into his car.

'Yes, that about wraps up our association for the time being, Gary,' said Howard as he got into his car and drove away before Bottrell could answer.

CHAPTER TWENTY

Mrs Hilda Baker was employed by Darrell Potter to clean his house and wash and iron his clothes every Wednesday and Friday morning. It was Wednesday, so she was surprised to see that his van was outside his house at nine o'clock. He'd usually gone, to wherever he went, before eight in the morning. She hoped he wouldn't be around all morning while she was cleaning. He was always criticising her work and getting in her way and she couldn't even take a short break to make a cup of tea. She disliked Potter intensely but cleaning jobs were hard to find in the deprived and run-down area where she lived.

She opened the front door with the key he had given her and made her sign a receipt for. She went into the sitting room, expecting him to be sitting there watching television or making out his betting slips. But he wasn't there. Next, she went into the kitchen. He wasn't there. Perhaps he's having a lie in, she thought, but that was unlikely on one of her days for cleaning. She called up the stairs—no answer. That's good, she could get on with her work in peace and even make herself as cup of tea and watch the telly while she took a break. She went to the cupboard under the stairs to collect the vacuum cleaner. She plugged it into a socket in the sitting room, but it was powerless. The fuse in the vacuum cleaner must have blown, she thought. She tried the television. It wasn't working, nor was the lamp behind his favourite armchair.

She spent an hour dusting and polishing in the sitting room and washing up the pile of dirty dishes and saucepans that Potter had left on the kitchen draining board.

Having done all she could downstairs, without electrical power, she went upstairs to make his bed, tidy his bedroom and the spare room, which was full of tools, rolls of electrical wiring and boxes of all manner of electrical equipment. As she crossed the landing, she noticed the power cable plugged into the socket. She followed the cable into the bathroom, let out a loud scream and dropped her tray of cleaning materials as she saw the ashen and distorted face and body of the half-submerged Potter in the bath. She knew he was dead and knew she couldn't bear to stay in the room a second longer. She dashed down the stairs to the sitting room, grabbed the telephone and with a trembling hand dialled 999.

When she was through to the local police control room she blurted out to the officer who answered, 'I've just found my employer dead in his bath!'

'What is your name and from where are you ringing?' asked the control room officer.

'I'm Mrs Hilda Baker and I'm ringing from Mr Potter's house. I'm his cleaner!' Hilda replied hysterically.

'Please calm down, madam, and tell me the address

from where you are speaking,' the officer said in a gentle voice.

'It's 52 Bartholomew Road; please hurry. This has made me come all over queer.'

'You must stay where you are until our officers arrive. They won't be long.'

Hilda put down the phone and sat looking at the blank television screen. Five minutes passed and there was a loud bang on the door. Hilda smoothed her hair into place, went to the door and opened it. Several uniformed and plainclothes police officers stood outside. A plainclothes officer stepped forward and displayed his warrant card. 'I'm Detective Inspector Rutledge and these are all police officers. We are here in response to a call made by a Mrs Hilda Baker from this address. Are you Mrs Baker?'

'Yes, Inspector, I made the call. It's Mr Potter, he's upstairs in the bathroom and I think he's dead.'

Rutledge entered and the other officers followed him into the sitting room.

'Lead the way then, Hilda,' said Rutledge.

Hilda gave a shudder and backed away. 'Oh... no, I don't want to look at him again.'

'I'm afraid it's necessary. Please lead the way,' said Rutledge in an authoritative tone.

Hilda walked to the foot of the stairs, followed by Rutledge, who motioned to two of the officers to follow him.

They entered the bathroom. Hilda stood back looking out of the window.

Rutledge looked at Potter's body and the electric fire

lying at the bottom of the bath. 'It looks like an accident, Barry,' he said to Detective Sergeant Loomis.

Loomis looked into the bath and saw the nail. 'Yes, certainly looks that way; the weight of the fire must have pulled the nail out of the wall. That was a daft thing to do, to hook a fire on a nail, not a rawl plug and screw. That made it an accident waiting to happen, boss.'

'Yes, very stupid for someone who works as an electrician,' interposed Acting Detective Sergeant Madden, from the doorway.

Rutledge and Loomis spun around. 'Do you know this man?' Rutledge said sharply.

'I know of him, sir, if he's Darrell Potter; he's a bit of a wide boy who calls himself an electrician and does bodge jobs for anyone who is unwary enough to hire him. Our collator has his name on file as someone who has come to our notice for dubious practices.'

'Yes, and I've never known him to have and electric fire in here before,' said Hilda.

Rutledge turned to her. 'Are you quite sure about that Mrs Baker?'

'Yes, I am Inspector. He had a rude picture hanging up where that hole in the wall is. I was in here last Friday and it was hanging up there then.'

Rutledge turned to Loomis. 'There's something very wrong here, Bob. This might be something more than an accident. Get on to the station and get the forensic team, the coroner's officer and a pathologist here ASAP.'

About twenty minutes later, a group of police officers,

led by Detective Chief Inspector Hawksworth and accompanied by a pathologist, arrived. A constable, who had been in the sitting room, admitted them.

'They're all upstairs, sir,' said the constable to Hawksworth.

Hawksworth acknowledged him with a nod and led the group up the stairs.

'What have we got here, then, Bob?' Hawksworth addressed Rutledge.

'This is Mrs Hilda Baker, sir. She works for the deceased as a cleaner. She came here this morning at nine and found Darrell Potter, who owns the house and is the only occupant, dead in the bath. He appears to have been electrocuted by that electric fire in the bath.'

'I can confirm that, Ron,' said the pathologist who had been examining the corpse.

Hawksworth looked up at the hole in the wall. 'That seems a rather dangerous place to hang an electric fire,' he observed.

'Yes, guv, it was, especially since Potter was an electrician. Mrs Baker told me that she'd never seen an electric fire in the bathroom and that a rude picture had been hanging in that position. The picture is now missing.'

Hawksworth turned to Mrs Baker, who was visibly shaking. 'Your information has been most helpful. Now you go downstairs with Barbara,' he said, pointing to a uniformed constable, 'and she will make you a nice cup of tea. If you feel unwell, our doctor will attend you.'

'Thank you, sir, you're very thoughtful,' said Hilda as she followed Barbara down to the kitchen. She'd get her cup of tea after all. The electric power might be off, but there was still the gas stove and an old kettle.

CHAPTER TWENTY ONE

Louise was laying the table for supper when the doorbell buzzed. 'That must be Tony,' she said, excitedly.

'I'll go,' said Larry dropping the evening paper on the sofa table.

'No, I'll go! I want to be the one to welcome him,' said Louise rushing to the front door.

Larry gave a secret smile and stood up to greet their guest. A minute later Louise entered the room with a tall, wavy-haired, fresh-faced man, who looked much younger than his 34 years. He was rather over-dressed for the occasion, wearing a grey business suit, white shirt and a Paisley tie. He's obviously trying to create a good first impression, thought Larry with a slight grin.

'This is Tony,' said Louise unnecessarily.

'I'm Larry,' said Larry, equally unnecessarily. 'I'm pleased to meet you, Tony,' he said extending his hand.

Tony responded with a firm grasp. 'I'm very pleased to meet you, too, Larry. Louise has told me what a father-like brother you've been for her. Your recent family tragedy must have been very upsetting for you both.'

'Yes, it was, Tony, but we've learnt how to put it in the past. Life must go on.'

'Now why don't you two sit down and let me get you a drink,' Louise said.

Larry sat in his favourite armchair, leaving the sofa for Tony to share with Louise.

'What would you like, Tony? I'm afraid we don't have much of a variety of drinks.'

'Oh… I'm not much of a drinker—anything will do me. I'll have what you or Larry is having.'

Louise gave a little laugh. 'That means it'll be either dubonnet and lemonade or dry sherry.'

'Hmm… I'm not at all familiar with dubonnet. Dry sherry will be fine. It is supposed to be an aperitif, isn't it?'

'Yes, that's right, but it's lost its appeal in recent years,' interposed Larry.

Louise poured the drinks and joined Tony on the sofa. 'Now before I order our meal, I'd like Tony to tell us all about his first day with the CID.'

'Yes, that would be interesting. I've always wanted to know how our police carry out their investigations,' said Larry, feigning a naivety about police business.

Tony was secretly delighted to talk about his new job. 'Well, I've had quite a first day as a CID aide. I was part of a team of detectives investigating the death of a man found electrocuted in his bath.'

'Wow, that was certainly a baptism of fire for you!' exclaimed Larry, grinning slyly. 'Do tell us all about it.'

'Oh… what a horrible experience for you on your first day in CID, but I suppose that's something our police have to expect,' said Louise. 'But please tell us all about your part in the investigation,' she added.

'To be perfectly honest, I was very small fry in the team. I was just supposed to watch and listen to what my experienced colleagues were doing and saying. It didn't take long for our DI to decide that it was almost certainly a case of foul play. Apparently, an electric fire that had been hanging on a nail over the bath had fallen into the water. The victim was said to be an electrician, who would surely not have placed an electric fire in such dangerous place.'

'Yes, it could hardly have been an accident. If it was murder, have any suspects come to light, or has a motive for the crime been established?' Larry asked.

'Well, at first it was thought that the relatives of an elderly man, who was electrocuted because of some shoddy work performed by the victim, had taken revenge. However, extensive enquiries indicated that Mr Haydon, that's the name of the elderly man who engaged Darrell Potter to do some rewiring for him, had no known friends or relations.'

'Ah—so Darrell Potter is the name of the electrician who was killed,' said Larry with a look of feigned surprise.

'Yes... er... that was his name. But you do realize, Larry, that what I am telling you is in the strictest confidence and shouldn't be repeated to anyone. But having said that, I expect most of what I have told you will be in the newspapers and on the television tomorrow.'

'Of course, he does. We both do. We wouldn't want you to get in any sort of trouble with your superiors,' Louise answered before Larry could reply.

'Anyone ready for another drink?' asked Larry, believing that he had gone as far as he should go in questioning Tony about the case.

'Please, no more drinks, Larry, I'm going to order our supper. What's it to be—Indian, Chinese or fish and chips?' said Louise, reaching for the telephone.

'I'd like Chinese, if that's all right with you,' said Tony.

'Yes, that's fine. We both like Chinese, so Chinese it will be,' said Louise, making a call to the local takeaway.

Within about five minutes the food arrived and Larry opened a bottle of dry white wine to accompany the meal.

During the meal Larry deliberately steered the conversation away from the Potter case and turned the conversation to the economy, the weather and holidays abroad. Tony could be a useful source of information about the progress of the investigation into Potter's death, but it wouldn't do for him to overdo his interest in the case.

CHAPTER TWENTY TWO

'The Chief is back from leave, guv, and he wants to see you ASAP,' said DI Rutledge with a trace of undisguised glee in his voice.

'DCI Hawksworth sighed deeply. 'Yes, I expect he does, Bob. So, you'd better get your troops out pronto looking for likely suspects.'

'If you're referring to the bloody cowboy builders' case, I have my entire section out following up on every lead we have,' replied Rutledge.

'Yes, and that's where you should be—leading from the front. Not stuck in your office, or swanning around headquarters all day.'

Hawksworth stalked off before Rutledge could think of an answer to his criticism.

Before reporting to Chief Superintendent Sharif, Hawksworth returned to his office to collect the four unsolved case files concerning the deaths of the five cowboy builders.

'Come in, Ron!' Sharif boomed in response to Hawksworth's deferential tap on his door.

Hawksworth was surprised to see that Superintendent

Lauren Armitage was sitting at the side of Sharif's desk. He hoped he might get some support from her, but her look of apprehension didn't bode well. Sharif had probably already taken her to task over the lack of progress made during his absence.

'Sit down, Ron, and tell me all about the progress *you haven't made* in clearing up these outstanding cases.'

Hawksworth sat down and arranged the case files in a neat pile on his knees, while he thought of something to say. 'I've every man we can spare out following up on all of the leads we have in these cases, sir.'

'Tell me, what leads are you following?'

'Well, we're now working on the assumption that there's some sort of struggle to get work going on between the cowboys. With all the publicity given out about cowboy builders on television and in the newspapers, members of the public are becoming more wary about whom they engage to do installation and repair work for them.'

'What a lot of nonsense, Ron! Surely you don't believe what you're saying? The people we're talking about might go as far as to bash each other over the head with hammers, but to go to all the trouble to burn alive, hang or electrocute their competitors is absolute balderdash! It's obvious to me that these killings have been well planned and, it seems, executed without leaving any clues that help your investigation. No, you'll have to come up with a more rational motive for the killings. I would suggest that revenge is the most likely motive.'

'Yes, sir, and I have had officers looking into that

possibility, but so far we've been unable to link any likely suspect to any of the murders.'

'Then perhaps we should be looking for some sort of crackpot taking revenge on behalf of the victims of these cowboy builders, Ron.'

'Yes, sir, we've already looked into that scenario, but these murders would have required at least two *crackpots* to carry them out. In this connection, I have assigned Acting Sergeant Madden to follow up on his hunch that two of the first victims of the cowboy builders are in some way linked. Although that is extremely unlikely, because they have nothing in common save the fact that they have both lost family members through the incompetence of the cowboy builders. And, oh yes, they have both served in the army, but in different regiments. However, they have iron-clad alibis for the time that those responsible for the deaths of their families were killed.'

Sharif shook his head and turned to the superintendent. 'What do you think about this, Lauren?'

'All I can say is that it is an extraordinary case, but I know that during your absence Ron has been tireless in his efforts to get it cleared up. However, I would suggest that the only link *needed* for them to get together is that they have both suffered at the hands of the cowboy builders. So, perhaps Ron should put more resources in support of Sergeant Madden's theory.'

'All right, let's hope that this may prove more rewarding, because I'm getting constant flak from the top brass over what they consider is incompetence in our handling of these cases. So, Ron, I want you to pull out all the stops and put every available detective and uniform officer on the case.'

'Very well, sir,' said Hawksworth, as he gathered up his files and left the office.

CHAPTER TWENTY THREE

It was about 8.30 in the evening and Larry and Louise were playing Scrabble. Louise had just made an eight-letter word and was crowing with delight, as she totalled her score, when the doorbell buzzed.

'Are you expecting anyone tonight, Louise?'

'No, Tony wouldn't turn up without first ringing me.'

'I'm not either, so I wonder who is disturbing us at this time of night.'

'You'll only find out if you answer the door,' said Louise with a laugh as Larry rose reluctantly to leave the room.

The door buzzed again as he opened it to reveal a man and a woman standing in the passageway. They look like coppers, he thought. This was confirmed as the man presented a police warrant card for inspection. 'I'm Acting Detective Sergeant Madden and this is Detective Constable Burnside,' he said, pointing over his shoulder to the young woman. 'May we come in, please?'

'Well, I suppose so, but what's this all about, Sergeant?'

'I'm sorry to disturb you at home, Mr Howard, but we

have one or two questions that we need to put to you.'

Larry stood aside to let them in and led them into the sitting room. Before Louise, who had a surprised look, could say anything, Larry introduced the two detectives. 'They have a couple of questions they want to ask me. Please sit down officers,' he said motioning to the sofa.

They both took out notebooks. Madden held his in a position to read and Burnside placed hers on her knees ready to take notes.

'Shall I leave you to it then, Larry?' said Louise, getting up from her chair.

Larry looked questioningly at Madden.

'I'd like you to be present when I question your brother, Miss Howard, because I might have something to ask you.'

'Very well,' Louise retorted and sat down.

Larry began to feel uneasy as he watched Madden reading his notes. 'Can we get this over quickly, Sergeant?'

'Yes, of course, I'll not hold up your game too long. Who's winning anyway?'

'My sister, as usual, but can we now have your questions, please?'

Madden shut his notebook and put it in his pocket. 'I understand that you served in the army for 22 years. During that time did you ever know a soldier called Gary Bottrell?'

Larry shook his head. 'No, I don't recall ever knowing anyone by that name.'

'He was a military policeman,' Madden went on.

Larry gave a short laugh. 'Thankfully, I never had much to do with Redcaps and there were about one-hundred and fifty thousand soldiers in the British Army when I was serving. I was a WO2 in the REME and looking back over my time in the army, I can only remember the names of about forty or fifty soldiers and they were mainly those in the REME and a few in infantry regiments.

'Are you absolutely positive that you never knew a Corporal Gary Bottrell?'

'Yes, I'm absolutely positive, that I didn't. Is that it, then, Sergeant?'

'No, not quite, sir. Can you tell me where you were between the hours of eight o'clock on the night of the 29th of April and six o'clock on the morning of the 30th of April?'

Larry grinned broadly. 'Off hand no, but I was most likely in bed from about 10.30 p.m. on April 29th to about 6.30 the following morning.'

'Is there anyone who can verify that?'

'Well, I seem to remember that Larry was here that evening fitting some units in my bedroom. And we usually go to bed after News at Ten,' interposed Louise.

'Is that correct, Mr Howard?'

'I really don't remember what I did that night, but if Louise is sure that I was here, then I was here! So, what's this all about, Sergeant—am I suspected of some kind of offence, because if I am I'd like to know what it is?'

Madden eyes narrowed. 'No, you are not being accused of any offence, we're just trying to establish certain facts concerning the death of a man called Reginald Meldrum, whose negligent work caused the death of a woman and her daughter we—'

'Oh, I remember that case,' interrupted Louise. 'I read about it in the paper. A man named Meldrum, described as a cowboy builder in the Press, failed to fit a carbon-dioxide monitor after fitting a new boiler and the poor woman and her daughter died. You must remember, Larry, we watched a news story about it on television. And, come to think of it, the woman and child who died were called Bottrell!'

'Your sister's got it bang on,' said Madden with a humourless laugh. 'They were Gary Bottrell's wife and daughter.'

'Okay, so what! How does that concern me?'

'Well, it seems it doesn't, but it surprises me that you didn't remember the name Bottrell, after having read about it in the paper and seen the television news about the case.'

'Yes, I put my hands up to that. Louise has a much better memory for facts and names than I have. That's probably something to do with her occupation as a teacher. Now is there anything else, Sergeant?'

'No, not at present, but I must mention that I spoke to your line manager, who told me that you had taken some leave a few days before the 29th April. I suppose that was to complete the alterations to your sister's bedroom?'

'Yes, that is so.'

Madden and Burnside stood up, ready to leave. 'Goodnight to you both. We're very sorry to have interrupted your game,' said Madden.

Larry led them to the front door. 'Goodnight, Sergeant, Constable,' he said as he closed the door on them and heaved a great sigh.

'Do you want to finish the game, Louise?' said Larry said as he entered the sitting room.

'No, I think I'd rather have a little talk with you about the interest the police have shown about your whereabouts on April 29th.'

'That was simply police routine. They always check the details of everyone who has any connection with the victim of a crime.'

'That's all very well, but why were they questioning you about your movements on the night that Meldrum was murdered? I can understand why they questioned you over the death of that man Capstick. They might have thought you'd killed him in revenge for the death of our parents. But surely they can't think you had anything to do with Meldrum's death!'

'No, of course not, but there's been quite a few deaths of so-called cowboy builders recently, so I expect the police have got their wires crossed somewhere and are investigating the possibility that these deaths are somehow connected. Anyway, they were quite satisfied with what you told them.'

'Yes, I agree, *but I'm not satisfied that you were here on the evening of 29th April*. So, perhaps you can tell me.'

'Oh, perhaps I wasn't. It might have been one of the nights when I was out with some of my old army pals.'

'Then why didn't you tell the police that? If you had done so they could have checked with them to confirm that you were with them on that night.'

'I'd forgotten where I was and I don't even know the addresses of any of our group. We just meet up in a pub and before we leave the pub we decide when we'll next meet. And, anyway, I didn't want any of my friends to be bothered with police enquiries.'

'Larry, I have the distinct feeling that you are withholding something from me and it's beginning to worry me.'

Larry put his arm around Louise's shoulder and drew her towards him. 'Now, you know that can't be true because I've always been straightforward with you and you know more about me than even mum and dad did. So, please stop interrogating me like you're a detective and I'm a prime suspect in a murder case. I'll make some cocoa and then I suggest we get a reasonably early night. I haven't mentioned it before, but I am a bit behind with my work and it may mean me having to do overtime to catch up.'

Louise pecked him on the cheek and drew away. 'Oh, I'm sorry to hear that. Perhaps that's why you've been a little bit touchy recently. You must get proper rest if you are under stress at work. So, get yourself to bed now and I'll make the cocoa.'

'Thanks, Lou,' he said, using her pet name, 'you're an

angel.' Larry hated himself for having to deceive her, but realized that in his present situation there was no alternative.

CHAPTER TWENTY FOUR

'Where are we going to now, Sarge?' DC Burnside said as she got into the driver's seat of their car.

'I think we'll pop in to see Gary Bottrell. It's his night off so he is likely to be in. You know the way, don't you, Terri?'

'Yes, but isn't it a bit late to call on anyone?'

'Yes, on normal people, but this man keeps odd hours. If it's a wasted journey we'll head back to the station to report to the DCI what we've learnt from Howard.'

'I didn't think we learnt anything from that interview,' Burnside said as she put the car into gear and drove off.

'Terri, my dear, when you've been in this game as long as I have you'll know to take more notice of what suspects don't tell you rather than what they do tell you! Howard was definitely trying to cover up where he had been on the night of the 29th. His sister got him off the hook, but I'm not sure whether that was her intention or that she simply made a mistake.'

'She struck me as being pretty straightforward and I don't think she was lying,' Burnside said as she weaved the car through the late evening traffic.

'Time will tell, Terri.'

Burnside braked outside Bottrell's apartment building. 'His flat is number 12, isn't it, Sarge?'

'That's it, Terri,' said Madden, joining her on the pavement.

He led the way up the grimy and littered stairway to the first floor. Ignoring the bell push he rapped loudly on the front door. A half a minute passed and no reply. He rapped again more loudly. A light came on in the hallway and Bottrell, dressed in a bathrobe, answered the door. He was bleary eyed and tousle haired. Recognising Madden, he snarled: 'What the fuck do you want now, copper? It's after ten and I've had a busy day.'

'Who is it, Gary?' a female called from the sitting room.

'It's the bloody cops again! You get back in bed; I shan't be long, Rita.'

'We have some questions that need answering, Mr Bottrell. Now, either you can invite us in or we can take you to the station. So, what's it to be?'

'You can't do that to me! I don't have to answer any of your questions without my brief being present.'

'That can be arranged at the station, but you will be under arrest.'

'Okay, come in and question away, I've nothing to hide!' He opened the door wide and Madden and Burnside entered and followed him into the sitting room. Rita Petchnik, dressed in an almost see-through silk dressing gown, was sitting in an armchair pouring vodka into a glass.

'I thought I told you to go back to bed, Rita!'

'I'd like Ms Petchnik to be present, if you don't mind, sir,' said Madden.

'Well, I do mind and I warn you, Madden, I shall put this matter into the hands of my solicitor.'

'I promise you Mr Bottrell, what I have to ask you won't take long. Have you ever met an ex-soldier named Laurence Howard?'

This was the cue for Burnside to take a notebook and a pen from her handbag.

'I don't know—I met lots of soldiers in my time as a military policeman. When I was based at the detention barracks at Colchester we got an intake of court-martialled soldiers every week, but I don't recall any of them being called Laurence Howard.'

'Where were you between the hours of nine o'clock and noon on the 18th of April?'

'I can't remember. I was probably in bed with Rita, sleeping off a night's duty at the club!'

Madden looked hard at Rita, who was refilling her glass. 'Well, was he, Ms Petchnik?'

'Yes, I do believe he was,' she answered with a smile.

'Would you be prepared to swear an oath on that?'

'Yes, I fucking well would, copper!'

'Have you any more questions for me, Detective Sergeant Madden?' said Bottrell with a sneer.

'Just one more—did you kill Steve Capstick?'

'Steve Capstick? I've never heard of him! Did you just make that name up?'

'No, he was a man who was bludgeoned and burnt to death in his van. I know you did it and I'm coming after you, Bottrell, and I'm going to nail you on a murder charge!'

'You'll bear witness to what's been said here tonight, by this detective, won't you, Rita?'

'I certainly shall, Gary. Now, can we get back to bed?'

'Yes, you run along, pet, while I see these police officers off the premises.'

'Don't bother, Mr Bottrell, we'll find our way out.'

'You stuck your neck out a bit with the way you spoke to Bottrell, Joe,' said Burnside as she and Madden got into their car. 'If he's got a good anti-police brief you might find yourself up on a disciplinary hearing.'

'He's got no brief to represent him. He's just full of bullshit and is as guilty as hell. I'll have him bang to rights for murder if it's the last thing I do before my retirement!'

'Well, I have to say it, Sarge, you do have a very unorthodox way of conducting police business.'

'Yes, Terri, perhaps I do, but it's necessary when you're dealing with suspects like Bottrell.'

CHAPTER TWENTY FIVE

When Howard got home from work, he found that Tony Jarvis was sitting on the sofa with Louise. The television wasn't on so he guessed that they had been deep in conversation or, perhaps, taking advantage of being alone, simply canoodling.

Tony got up as he entered. 'What sort of day have you had, Larry?'

'Much the same as I usually have. I'm sure your day has been much more interesting.'

'Shall I make some tea, or do you chaps want a drink before dinner?' said Louise getting up from the sofa and smoothing her dress.

'Yes, tea will be fine for me. Are you okay with that Tony?' said Larry, picking up the evening paper and sitting in his fireside chair.

'Yes, thanks, I'd rather not drink tonight. I'm back on again at six in the morning and might be required to do a double shift.'

'So you're settling in with your new job?'

'Yes, and my section commander is getting me more involved in our current investigation.'

'What's that, if it's all right for me to ask?'

'Oh, we're still dealing with the cowboy builders' case, but I was called away this morning to assist with a case of suicide. Coincidentally, it's connected with another cowboy builder. I noticed that there's a report in the evening paper about it.'

'Oh, really? Cowboy builders are certainly in the news these days,' said Larry with a short laugh.

Louise brought the tea tray in and poured the tea while Larry and Tony discussed the growing crime rate in certain parts of the country.

'I have read the evening paper's version of the story, but do tell us all about your part in the investigation, Tony,' Louise said as she laid the table.

'The report of it in the evening paper is not complete. That's because we can't give the media too much information about a case that's still under investigation,' said Tony.

'Yes, it's known that the police do like to keep things close to their chests,' said Larry.

'Only if it's in the public's interest to do so,' replied Tony, wearing a hurt look.

'If you're ready to eat, I'll bring the food in,' said Louise.

Without a word, Larry and Tony sat down at the dining table—a hint enough for Louise to return to the kitchen.

During their meal, Larry deliberately steered the table talk away from the cowboy builders' investigations. 'Have you seen any good films lately, Tony?' he asked, knowing that Louise, who was a modern film buff, would welcome the subject and given the chance would keep it going throughout the evening.

'I don't find the time to go to the cinema much these days, but recently I've seen one or two good films on my television.'

'Such as?' Larry said to keep the conversation going.

'I bought the DVD, *Harry Brown,* because Michael Caine was in it and he's a favourite of mine. He played a very different role, but I quite enjoyed it.'

'I saw that film, Tony,' said Louise, 'I thought it very grim. It rather overstated the way our young people are involved in drug abuse and the firearms they seem able to obtain. What surprised me was that Michael Caine's Harry Brown was never brought to book for the young people he killed.'

'Yes, that sort of ending to a film can be a bad influence for the young,' Tony agreed. 'It can lead them to think that almost any crime can be justified. It would be much better if film-makers made sure that the end of such films always showed that crime doesn't pay and that offenders are always brought to justice.'

'There's not much hope of that happening, Tony,' Larry said. 'The film-loving public is beginning to develop a sneaking regard for errant anti-heroes. That's why films like *Harry Brown, The Getaway, The Thomas Crown Affair, Butch Cassidy and the Sundance Kid, Point Blank,* Michael Winner's *Death Wish* series, *The Tom Ripley* films, and many more like them have proved to be popular with the general public.'

'I have to admit that I've enjoyed most of those films, but they do give a misguided influence to the impressionable youth,' said Tony.

'Yes, and although most of them carry a restricted viewing rating, very young children do get to see them on DVDs in their home. I'm very surprised with what I hear from the children talking about what they have seen and the appalling language they've heard in some of the recent films,' said Louise.

'Well, Louise, Larry, I suppose I'd better be pushing off if I'm to get an early night. Thank you for the splendid meal, Louise,' said Tony, rising from the table.

'When will we see you again, Tony?' Louise said. 'You are always welcome, isn't he Larry?'

'Yes, of course, he is,' Larry replied.

Louise led Tony to the front door and they spent several minutes saying their goodnight in the hallway. They must be getting very fond of each other, thought Larry. It would be a shame if anything happened to spoil their relationship. I'd be quite happy to see Louise married and have Tony as a brother-in-law.

'Do you fancy a nightcap, Larry?' said Louise, on returning to the sitting room.

'Do you mean cocoa?'

'Of course, what else did you think I meant? You did drink most of the wine and ended the meal with a brandy. Don't you think that's enough alcohol for one evening?'

'Yes, and I don't want any cocoa, thank you. I think I'll turn in with the newspaper. I didn't get a chance to read it this evening.'

'I think I'll follow suit when I've cleared the table and done the dishes. I've got a busy schedule tomorrow. Goodnight Larry.'

'Do you want me to help?'

'No thanks, Larry. I know you're itching to read that story about the woman who committed suicide because she was being harassed by cowboy builders. I read it before you came home and found it very moving. Those evil men treated that poor woman so badly that she was driven to take her own life. I hope those responsible get a custodial sentence.'

'Yes, I couldn't agree more, Louise. Goodnight,' Larry said, picking up the newspaper as he left the room.

In bed with a glass of brandy on his bedside locker and the evening newspaper spread out on the duvet, he turned the pages until he found the story he wanted. It read:

Victim of Cowboy Builders Commits Suicide

Mrs Ruby Devonish, 62, a retired pharmacist, of Lewisham, was found dead in her home by her sister, Mrs Ivy Garside. A post-mortem examination indicated that she had committed suicide by taking poison. Mrs Garside told the Coroner's Court that her sister had paid £55,000 up front to a firm of builders to carry a modernisation of her home. The builders started the work, but abandoned the site when Mrs Devonish refused to pay them any more money until the work was completed. The house was left in a turmoil and almost uninhabitable; with floor boards ripped up, internal doors removed, external doors left insecure, leaks through the roof, electrical wiring left unsafe and holes knocked through internal walls. Mrs Garside said that because of what had happened her sister was suffering from severe depression, which might have caused her to commit suicide. A police representative told our reporter that the matter is being investigated.

This is certainly a matter that requires my attention, Howard thought as he sipped his brandy. But how am I to find out the names of the men who caused Mrs Devonish so much misery, which led to her suicide? Perhaps I can find out what I want from Mrs Garside. That's if I am able to locate her. If I did, I should have to impersonate a police officer. Although, if I were able to convince her that I was a policeman, it would probably prove fruitless, because no doubt she has already told the police everything she knows about the builders who were working on her sister's house. Not only that, but she might even inform the police of my visit. The police would then get my description from her and it wouldn't be long before they were calling on me again to find out why I was interested enough in the matter to impersonate a policeman to obtain information about something that was of no concern of mine. No, I must give my next move careful consideration before I do anything else. With that in mind, Howard finished his brandy and fell into a fitful sleep.

CHAPTER TWENTY SIX

Howard got up at six o'clock, turned his computer on and set it up to print business cards. He printed three in the name of *Charles Tindall, Staff Reporter, Lewisham and District Chronicle,* with a false telephone number, website and email address.

He joined Louise for their usual hurried breakfast, when they talked briefly about Tony's visit the previous evening and when he might make his next visit.

At midday, when he usually took his lunch break, Howard went to the office, which held the Electoral Roll for the borough. It took him about half an hour to find Mrs Devonish's address: 34 Tarleton Avenue. He returned to his office and told his assistant that he would be spending most of the afternoon checking the work in progress at one of the sites he was overseeing.

He drove to Tarleton Road, which was made up with semi-detached houses, and parked several houses past number 34. He walked back to number 32 and knocked on the door. A mumsy looking woman of about sixty opened the door. Before she could say anything, Howard produced one of his business cards and handed it to her.

Then, with the most pleasing smile he could muster, said: 'Good morning madam, I do hope I've not caught you at a bad time,' and added, noting that she held a duster in her left hand, 'but I would like to have a few words with you about your former neighbour, Mrs Ruby Devonish.'

The woman read the card and handed it back to him. 'So, you're a reporter, eh? Well, I am busy at the moment,' she said, hastily putting the duster on the hall table, 'but I can spare you a few minutes. Please come in.'

The woman led Howard into her sitting room, which was sparsely furnished, but cosy and inviting with a strong smell of lavender. 'Please sit down, Mr Tindall,' she said with a smile and sat opposite Howard.

I think she's taken a shine to me, thought Howard. That should make questioning her easier.

'Being immediate neighbours, I imagine you knew Mrs Devonish quite well.'

'Oh, yes, we were very close friends. We were both widows, so we spent a lot of time together. We even went on holidays together. I was so upset when she died. Will you be putting what I tell you into your newspaper?'

'Only if you agree to that and if you do we will pay you for your story.'

'Oh, I didn't know that. I'm not very good at putting words together. You ask me what you want to know and I'll do my best to answer you. Before you start, would you like a cup of tea or coffee?'

'No thank you, madam. It's very kind of you to offer, but I don't want to put you to any trouble.'

'Please don't call me madam. My name is Florence Hogan, and all my friends and neighbours call me Flo.

She's obviously very lonely and just wants someone to talk to, thought Howard. 'Okay, Flo, can you tell me the name of the firm that did the work on her house?'

'Well, yes, I did write it down when she told me who was doing her work, but after seeing what they've done to her house and giving her all that hassle over money, I wouldn't give them the job of making a rabbit hutch!'

Flo went to her sideboard and took out a notebook. She opened it and read: '*Harkness and Thompson. Trust us to modernise your home. We guarantee all our work. Tel: 78018-643746.* For what they did they ought to be locked up for good! There's no doubt that they were responsible for causing poor Ruby to end her life.'

Flo handed Howard the notebook. He quickly jotted down the details in his diary and handed the notebook back. 'You've been very helpful Flo. I take it you have no objection to what you have told me being published?'

'Oh, no, that'll be fine, Mr Tindall. I'll look forward to seeing it. Now you did mention that you paid for news stories?'

'Yes, I did. We normally pay about a hundred pounds, by cheque, for a good news story, but I can't guarantee that your news item will be published. That's always the editor's decision and depends on what space is available in our next edition. However, as you have been so helpful I am going to pay you an advance in cash. If your story is not published, you can keep the money anyway. Is that all right for you?'

'Yes, that's very good of you. It will save me going to the bank.'

Howard took out his wallet and took out two twenty-pound notes. 'Here you are, Flo,' He said handing her the cash.

'Thank you Mr Tindall. Now are you sure you don't want a cuppa before you leave?'

'No thanks, Flo, I'm afraid I've got to dash back to the office, to write up your story,' Howard said, standing up and walking to the door.

Flo led him to the front door. 'Thank you very much, Mr Tindall,' she said, opening the door.

'Goodbye, Flo,' Howard replied with a warm smile.

* * * * *

Howard went to Blackheath station and tapped in Harkness and Thompson's mobile phone number. A coarse voice answered, 'Hello, who's that?'

'Is that Mr Harkness?' Howard replied.

'No, it ain't, he's out on a job.'

'Are you Mr Thompson?'

'Yes, that's me. What do you want, mate?'

'My name is Robert Arkwright and I'd like to discuss plans to have some upgrading done to my house. Would it be possible for me to come to see you and your partner at your office?'

'We don't have an office. We work from home, or in our yard at the back of the house.'

'Well, may I visit you at your home?'

'I suppose so, but we usually do business at the place where the job is.'

'Yes, I quite understand that, but I'm afraid it's not convenient to conduct business in my home at the present time. So, can we arrange a mutually convenient time for my brother and I to call at your home? I have full details of my requirements for you to study and I am prepared to pay well if the job can be completed in about two weeks.'

'Okay, I'll speak to my partner. It'll have to be on an evening.'

'That's fine. So, shall we say tomorrow evening at about eight?'

'Yeah, that'll be all right. There's just one thing though—we'll need an up-front advance, in cash, before we start the job.'

Howard gave a short humourless laugh. 'Yes, I wouldn't expect you to make any other sort of arrangement. All I need now is your address.'

'It's 23 Milton Street, Lewisham. Our van will be parked outside.'

'Good, we'll call on you at eight tomorrow evening then.'

'Cheers, mate. We'll see you tomorrow evening then,' Thompson said.

Howard put down the phone and then rang Bottrell. He's probably in bed with that sluttish whore, thought Howard as he waited two minutes for the phone to be answered.

'Now what do you want, Howard? I thought we'd ended our business arrangement.'

'I need your help to deal with two more cowboys. You must have read or seen the story of the old woman who committed suicide because of the harassment she got from two of those scumbags.'

'Yes, it made me cry my eyes out, pal,' Bottrell replied sarcastically.

'You're all heart, Gary. I bet you left the Redcaps because you couldn't bear to see prisoners suffering from the nasty physical attentions of people like you at Colchester.'

'Now listen, Howard, there's only one way you'll get any more help from me, and that is to hand over that tape before we do anything else.'

'All right, that's a deal. I'll bring it to our usual meeting point and hand it over before we move off. I've told our targets that we'll call on them at eight o'clock tomorrow evening. So they'll be in waiting. Their address is 23 Milton Street, Lewisham. You can't miss it because they leave their white van outside. Wear your disguise, we can't risk being seen by neighbours who might be questioned by the police to describe any strangers seen in the vicinity. I haven't made any firm plans as to how we'll deal with them, but whatever it is they'll not be in business much longer. In case they prove to be hard men to manage, you'd better bring your little persuader with you.'

'You mean my cosh? I've got something much more useful than that to use as a *persuader*!'

'What's that then?'

'It's a Webley and Scott Mark 6, point 455 calibre revolver. I've also have twelve rounds of ammo for it.'

'How the hell did you get one of those?'

'Never mind how I got it! It's not traceable and it'll give us a good edge in dealing with any sort of opposition.'

'I don't like the idea of using firearms to achieve our purpose. If they're not properly handled they can be a danger to the general public.'

'There's nothing to worry about on that score. I passed out as a marksman with small arms on my military police course. Anyway, bad cowboys do get shot by lawman, don't they,' Bottrell said with an almost hysterical laugh.

'This is not some sort of Wild West cowboys and Indians game we're playing, Bottrell. It's what I hope will be seen by many as a service to the old, the vulnerable and the unwary.'

'Okay, Sheriff, I'll try to keep that in mind and see you at eight tomorrow evening,' Bottrell said and switched off his phone.

I think it is definitely time to part time with Bottrell, Howard thought as he drove back to his office. He seems to be losing his marbles and now even *enjoying* what he's doing. That's quite wrong and could prove to be dangerous.

CHAPTER TWENTY SEVEN

'Have you got any plans for this evening, Louise?' Larry said as he was about to leave for work.

'Yes, Tony's taking me to the theatre. I don't know which one, so I don't know what we'll be seeing. He said it was to be a surprise. He's picking me up at seven to take me for what he describes as a special meal and then to the theatre. I sense that it may be the setting for him to produce an engagement ring, or even a proposal of marriage! I thought I'd already told you that I was going out this evening. I apologise if I didn't.'

'If you did, I can't understand how I forgot such unexpected, but nevertheless wonderful news!'

'I'm glad you're pleased about my news, Larry. What are your plans for this evening?'

'The Michael Caine film, *Harry Brown*, which Tony recommended and I've been waiting to see on television, is on tonight, so I'm staying in to watch it.'

'Well, I'll not be back until about 11.30, Larry, so don't bother to wait up for me. I'll see you at breakfast to tell you all about the show and everything else that happened.'

'I'll look forward to that, Louise. Cheerio,' Larry said as he left the flat.

* * * * *

As soon as Tony had called and left with Louise, Larry collected his disguise from the boot of his car and put it on. He collected the tape he had made of his first conversation with Bottrell and put it in the inside pocket of his raincoat.

He left at 7.30 and stopped at a shop, which sold DVDs. He bought the *Harry Brown* DVD and put it in the car door pocket.

Driving to Milton Street, he thought about Louise's news. He was pleased for her and felt that she and Tony Jarvis were a good match and that if they did decide to get married he must make sure that none of his homicidal activities came to light. If they did, Louise and Tony might be unable to marry, if Tony wanted to remain in the police force. Louise's career as a teacher might also be in jeopardy. Even if they settled for an informal relationship, their association with a murderer, which was what he was, might seriously damage their career prospects.

Arriving in Milton Street, Howard saw Bottrell's car parked a few yards beyond Harkness and Thompson's van. He drove a few yards beyond Bottrell's car, parked and got out. He went to Bottrell's car and saw that Bottrell was sitting in the car drinking from a bottle of whisky, seemingly oblivious of Howard's presence. Howard rapped on the window. Bottrell wound down the window and said, in a slurred voice: 'Where the fuck have you been? I've been waiting ages for you!'

'Get out of the car, you damned fool! I said we'd meet here at eight and it's only five to eight now!'

'Okay, okay, so my watch is a bit fast,' Bottrell said as he put the bottle of whisky under his seat, got out of the car and joined Howard on the dimly lit street. 'I hope you remembered to bring that tape.'

'Yes, I did, and you'll get it as soon as we've finished what we came here to do. Now don't speak unless you have to and keep your voice low. We don't want any nosey neighbours looking out of their windows when we approach number 23,' Howard said as he led the way.

Howard rang the doorbell and the door was opened almost immediately by a short, overweight man of about 35, who was dressed in worn jeans and what had once been a white tee shirt. 'Are you Mr Arkwright?' he said.

'Yes, I'm Robert Arkwright and this is my brother Rupert,' replied Howard, with a secret smile at the name he had given Bottrell.

'I'm Ben Thompson and my partner, Gerry Harkness is inside. So, come in, gents, and let's get down to business.'

Howard and Bottrell followed Thompson into an untidy and an unpleasantly smelling sitting room. Harkness, a balding, stubble faced man in his mid-thirties, dressed in tatty jeans and a paint-spattered tee shirt, was slumped on a sagging settee. He was watching a football match on a forty-two inch television in a corner of the room. The volume was so loud that conversation would have been nigh impossible without shouting. Thompson switched it off and turned to Harkness. 'We can't have that on when we're discussing business, Gerry.'

'Can't you just put it on mute so that we can see the match?'

'No, it's too distracting and we've got a lot to talk about. These gents want a full modernisation job done on their house.'

Harkness stood up. 'All right, Ben,' he replied. Then, to Howard and Bottrell, 'Sit here,' he said, pointing to the settee. Howard and Bottrell ignored his offer and chose to sit on two dining chairs, which were set against the wall, near the door. Much better seating to move from, when the need arose. Thompson joined Harkness on the settee.

'Well, Bob, did you bring your plan with you,' Thompson said, addressing Howard, who winced at his familiarity.

Howard shook his head and smiled grimly. 'No, we've come here tonight to talk about the modernisation of Mrs Devonish's house. You remember that job, which created so many problems for that dear old lady that she committed suicide.'

Thompson and Harkness looked at each other in bewilderment, then at Howard. 'What's that got to do with you?' Thompson said. 'It wasn't our fault that she topped herself. The silly old bitch didn't know what she wanted and wasn't prepared to pay the full price for the job.'

'From what I know about the mutual arrangement, was that she advanced you fifty-five thousand pounds, which was more than enough to cover the materials and time needed to do the job. You then hassled her for more money, which she could ill-afford. Are you proud of yourselves for the way you treated that woman?'

Harkness struggled up from the settee. His eyes bulged and his face was livid with rage. 'Who the bloody hell do you two old farts think you are, coming here and questioning us about our contracts? You can both piss off before we sort you out!'

Bottrell leaned forward and his right hand went into his raincoat pocket and withdrew a revolver, which he pointed at Harkness. 'Now you can both shut your foul mouths, get off your arses, get out of here and into your van.' He looked at Howard for confirmation.

Howard nodded. 'Yes, Gary, we've wasted enough time with these two and we're not likely to hear them apologising for what they've done or showing any compassion for their victim. If you're going to accompany them in the van, you'll know the sort of destination we want. I'll drive behind in my car. When we return, Gary, you can pick up your car.'

'Roger, Chief,' Bottrell said with a laugh.

Outside Bottrell ordered Thompson to take the wheel and told Harkness to sit next to him.

He sat next to Harkness with his revolver pressed into Harkness's side.

'Head for Bostall Woods,' Bottrell ordered Thompson.

Thompson made no reply as her drove off.

'Where the fuck are you taking us?' Harkness snarled.

Bottrell's only reply was to poke him savagely in the ribs with his revolver.

Howard followed the van a couple of car lengths behind.

It was about nine when they reached the road bordering Bostall Woods. There were few vehicles and no pedestrians using the dimly lit road.

'Park the van over there,' Bottrell ordered, pointing to a patch of open ground, which led into the woods.

Thompson complied, thinking that Bottrell intended driving off in their van and leaving them to walk home.

Howard stopped opposite the van, wondering what Bottrell planned to do next, when two shots rang out. He got out of the car and walked to the van. Bottrell was standing next to the van and removing the cap from the petrol tank.

'Get back in your car, Larry, I can manage what needs to be done on my own. You'd better drive a few yards back down the road and get ready for a quick getaway.'

Bottrell pulled his handkerchief from his pocket and lowered it into the petrol tank. He stopped what he was doing as an elderly man with a dog on a lead came out of the woods.

'Did you hear those shots, mate?' he said.

'Yes,' answered Bottrell with a laugh, 'probably just a couple of lads hunting rabbits.'

'You've not broken down, have you?' asked the man.

'No, I'm just having a break to stretch my legs. I've been on the road for hours—all the way from Carlisle.'

'Bloody hell, what a way to make a living,' said the man, as he walked off with his shaggy haired mongrel straining on its lead.

Bottrell waited until the man was out of sight and returned the petrol soaked handkerchief to the petrol tank. He pulled the handkerchief half out of the tank and lit the end with a match.

He waited until the flame was halfway down the handkerchief then ran the ten yards to where Howard had parked. He leapt into the car and as he slammed the door, there was a tremendous explosion. He looked back to see that the van was enveloped in flames. Howard drove off at speed. As they passed the man with the dog, Bottrell ducked his head.

'I really do believe you're enjoying our mission, Gary. I hope those two poor sods were dead when you fired the van.'

'Well, I put a well-placed bullet in both heads, so I expect they were.'

'You're a pretty callous bastard, Gary,' Howard said and reached into his pocket and withdrew the tape and passed it to Bottrell.

Bottrell took it and put it in his jacket inside pocket. 'Yes, I suppose I am,' he said with a smirk.

'You were wise to duck down when we passed that old chap with the dog. If he'd connected my car with the exploding van, and described it to the police, they wouldn't take too long to identify me. They'll know straightaway that the cowboy builders, who were probably known to them, had fallen victims to the vigilantes who've been eliminating cowboy builders. Our *modus operandi* will be familiar to them as well. I think we'd better go to ground for a few months before we take on any more missions.'

'Yes, perhaps you're right about that, but what you now need to know is that in future I shall be calling the shots!'

'How do you make that out?'

'Because, while you were taping our first conversations, so was I, Larry!'

'Damn you, Gary, I should have known that you would do something like that!'

'Well, I was just protecting my back, the same as you were.'

'Speaking of protecting backs, have you got an alibi for tonight?'

'I've always got one—Rita. She could lie for England in more ways than one! What about you?'

'Yes, I have provided myself with an alibi, which I shall keep to myself, until the police decide to question me again, as I'm sure they will. Now, if you don't mind, no more about it tonight and let me get back home before my sister gets back from her outing,' Howard said, pressing his foot down hard on the accelerator.

* * * * *

Back at the flat, Howard changed his clothes and put his disguise materials in the car boot. He took the DVD up to his bedroom and inserted it into his player, connected his earphones to the television and switched the set on. It was 9.45, so after he had fast-forwarded the forthcoming film trailers the film would run for 99 minutes and be finished before Louise got home at 11.30. It really didn't matter if it didn't, because he would turn off the bedroom light and as there was no sound coming from the television she would think he was asleep and wouldn't disturb him. As it happened the film ended before Louise got in at 11.45. Howard heard her saying goodnight to Tony at the front door. He hid the DVD in a suitcase he kept on the top shelf of his wardrobe, undressed, finished his brandy and went to sleep thinking about what he had to do in the morning.

CHAPTER TWENTY EIGHT

'Well, how did everything go last night?' Larry asked as Louise joined him at the breakfast table.

'Wonderfully, we had a splendid meal, accompanied by champagne and fine wine. The show was *Les Miserables*, which I had seen before, but still enjoyed it. But the high spot of the evening was Tony's proposal of marriage—and look at this,' Louise said, displaying her left hand across the table. Larry looked admiringly at the sparkling cluster of diamonds set in platinum.

'It's a lovely engagement ring, Louise. Am I to take it that Tony bought it without you being there to choose what you wanted?'

'Yes, it was a complete surprise!'

'From the expression on your face I can see that you are highly pleased with his choice.'

'I am, I am very pleased with it.'

'So when is the happy day to be?'

'It's to be on the first Saturday in June. I suppose you realize, you'll have to give me away? So, you'd better order a new suit.'

'Yes, I'll have to do the father bit,' Larry said, but he wondered if he'd be available.

'However, putting all that aside for the moment, Larry, I have to say that you don't look as though you had very much sleep last night. You're not going down with something, are you?'

'No, but I seem to be experiencing a bout of depression. I haven't mentioned it before, but things aren't going very well at work. I'm slipping behind with some of the contracts I oversee. Then there's all the trouble we're having with the insurance company. They seem to be doing their utmost to wriggle out of paying out our claim. If our claim were to be paid in full it would provide enough capital to invest in a home for you and Tony.'

'Larry, you must see your doctor straightaway. Perhaps what you need is a tonic and a few days off work. Don't worry about a home for us. Tony rents a very nice two bedroom flat and with what we've both saved we'd have enough to put down a sufficient deposit to raise a mortgage for a house.'

'Yes, perhaps you're right. As soon as you leave for work, I'll let my boss know that I'll not be in and then make an appointment to see my doctor. Now let's get back to talking about your wedding plans,' Larry said with a strained smile.

* * * * *

As soon as Louise left the flat, Larry rang his line manager. 'I'm afraid I'll not be in today, Geoff, I'm really under the weather, so I'm seeing my doctor today.'

'I'm sorry to hear that, Larry. You seem to be on top of everything in the department.'

'Yes, that's right, but I have a number of personal problems to deal with. I'm having difficulties getting our insurance claim settled. And, as you know, my sister is living with me and we seem to be on top of each other. I suppose it's because I've been used to living on my own. Now, she tells me she's getting married in a few weeks and she'll expect her husband to live in my flat until she can get somewhere else to live. So, I'm spending all my spare time trying to find alternative accommodation for them. Anyway, I'll let you know how I get on with the doctor.'

'Okay, Larry, don't worry about what's happening here; everything's going swimmingly, thanks to your efforts. Cheerio, Larry.'

Next, Howard rang his doctor and was fortunate enough to get an appointment for the early afternoon.

'Good afternoon, Mr Howard, what seems to be the trouble?' asked his doctor.

'It's difficult to explain, doctor. I seem to be in a state of deep depression and can't shake myself out of it. I'm experiencing problems at work and at home, which are causing me to be disagreeable, bad tempered and affecting my sleep, which is disturbed by the most horrific nightmares. And, to cap it all, I find it difficult to get over the tragic circumstances of the death of my parents. To put it bluntly I'm at my wits' end to deal with the simplest of problems.'

The doctor checked Howard's medical history on his

computer. 'There's nothing in your medical history to indicate that you have experienced anything before, like you've described. But then your army medical history is not yet included with our records. So, our records are incomplete. Did you suffer any bouts of depression when you were in the army?'

'Yes, I suppose I did—caused by my active service in Iraq and Afghanistan. I felt that our military involvement in the invasion of these two countries was futile and needless. The carnage I witnessed caused me much distress, but I withheld this reaction from my superiors.'

'Ah, now we are getting to the root of your problem. You are suffering from post-traumatic stress disorder, which you have been trying to suppress.'

'Is there anything that can be done to provide me with some relief, doctor?'

The doctor looked thoughtful for a moment or two, then asked: 'How would you describe your intake of alcohol?'

Howard gave a little laugh. 'Oh, I like the odd glass or two of brandy after my evening meal,' he said.

'How long have you been doing that?'

'About twenty to twenty-five years. That's not excessive, is it?'

'No, but strong spirits can have an adverse effect on your liver.'

'But as far as I know there's nothing wrong with my liver.'

'That may be so, but I am going to prescribe anti-depressant drugs for you that can have unpleasant side effects, particularly if you have any traces of liver disorder.'

'Well, I'll cut down on my intake of brandy while I'm taking the drugs. Will that help?'

'Yes, that would be ideal. The drug I'm prescribing is called Prozac. On no account should you take any other drug while you are taking Prozac.'

'Would that rule out the use of Paracetamol tablets, doctor?'

'Yes, it certainly would. I am prescribing a month's supply of Prozac. Come and see me again in four weeks,' the doctor said as he filled out a prescription and handed it to Howard.

Howard took the prescription to his local pharmacy and collected the prescribed tablets. The pharmacist warned him about taking any other drugs while he was taking those.

'The doctor told me all about that, but thank you,' he said with a smile.

CHAPTER TWENTY NINE

DCI Hawksworth and DI Rutledge were closeted with Chief Superintendent Sharif to brief him about the murder of two men near Bostall Woods.

'What have you come up with regarding these murders, Ron?'

Hawksworth consulted a file on his lap. 'The victims were both shot in the back of the head as they sat in the cab of their van. The van had been set alight and exploded. Both men were badly burnt and unrecognisable. However, from checks we've made of the vehicle we're pretty sure that the men were Ben Thompson and Gerry Harkness. These two were self-employed general builders. In fact, they were the two cowboy builders, to use the popular term, who made such a mess of modernising the house belonging to Mrs Ruby Devonish, that she committed suicide. In this connection, a file has already been submitted to the Crown Prosecution Service, to lay a charge against them. We're still awaiting a response to that, but you know how it is with the CPS, they'll not proceed unless they feel a hundred per cent sure that they can get a conviction.'

'Yes, we all know about that, Ron. CPS will now, I'm sure, be pleased to learn that they won't need to take a decision about them. But what I want to hear is how far are you away from coming up with the identity of the killer, or killers?'

'Harold Robson, the man, who called 999 to report the incident, had been walking his dog in Bostall Woods. He said that he had heard two shots and had spoken to a man who was standing near the van, who said that the shooting was probably a "couple of lads hunting rabbits." The man also told him that he was stretching his legs after having driven from Carlisle. I—'

'It's as plain as a pikestaff, Ron, that the man standing by the van was the killer! Did you get a description from Robson?'

Hawksworth looked down at his file. 'Yes, sir, but it wasn't very helpful. It was quite dark at the time.'

'Well, what did Robson see?' Sharif almost shouted, his short-temper beginning to show.

'He said the man was at least six feet tall, heavily built, probably in his sixties, with a straggly beard and wearing thick horn-rimmed glasses. He was wearing a shabby raincoat and a tweed cap. He spoke with a London accent.'

'Does that sound like he was a long-distance driver?'

'No sir, the driver was the dead man sitting behind the wheel in the van.'

'Exactly, Ron, so he must have been the killer. A

younger man than was described, in disguise, who had travelled with the two men, from wherever they came. Shot them and set fire to their van. What does need explaining is how did he leave the scene? He must have had a vehicle parked nearby. But if he had, who had driven it to Bostall Woods? He couldn't have done because he must have been in the van, and, with the threat of his gun, telling the driver to drive to a lonely spot where he could kill him and his mate. So what does all this suggest to you, Ron?'

'He must have had an accomplice, sir, who followed the van,' Rutledge interposed, before Hawkswoth could answer, which earned him a glare from Hawksworth.

Sharif smiled benignly at Rutledge. 'Good, now we're getting somewhere.'

'Although it may have no significance, sir, but the man with the dog said he saw a car driving away at speed from nearby, immediately after the explosion. He glanced at the car and saw only the driver. He was unable to give a description other than to say that he was of slighter build than the man he'd seen at the van. He didn't see the car registration.'

'Then I suggest that he saw the getaway car. The killer would have had the presence of mind to duck down as they passed the man with the dog. It's a pity the man with the dog—Robson—didn't get the car's registration number, or even its make.'

'He did say that he thought it was a light coloured car, possibly silver grey,' interposed Rutledge.

'That's too popular a colour for us to check every car of that description, sir,' said Hawksworth.

'Yes, I agree, so where does that leave us? I'm inclined to believe that we are looking for at least two men, possible relatives, bent on revenge for the death of the late Mrs Devonish. But I find it hard to believe that the same men are responsible for all the murders. What worries me is that firearms are now being used. By the way, has Acting Sergeant Madden come up with anything new on his theory that all the murders are being carried out by those two ex-soldiers, Howard and Bottrell?'

'No, sir, but I have given him carte blanche to carry out his inquiries. No doubt he'll be visiting those two men to check that they both have alibis.'

'If you want my opinion, sir,' Rutledge interposed, 'I think Madden is wasting his time following up on his half-baked idea. It occurs to me that there might be some sort of rivalry going on between the cowboy builders. After all, with the publicity they've been given in the newspapers and on the television they may be finding it hard to find people stupid enough to give them work. So, they are fighting each other for the work that's available.'

'Inspector Rutledge, I did not ask for, nor do I want to hear, your absurd opinion! This is not some sort of range war being fought by cowboys. You'll be suggesting next that Billy the Kid is responsible for all the killings. I also find that your denigration of the vulnerable and unwary of the practices of these cowboy builders, to be in the worst possible taste! Now both of you get back on the job and make some arrests. Even the Commissioner is taking a close interest in this case and wants to know why we are, as he puts it, "stuck in a mire of indecision".'

CHAPTER THIRTY

'What did the doctor have to say?' Louise asked Larry at the breakfast table.

Larry paused from spreading marmalade on his toast. 'Oh, aside from the minor problems that beset me at the moment, such as the trouble we are having over our insurance claim, he diagnosed that I was suffering from suppressed post-traumatic stress disorder caused by my experiences in Iraq and Afghanistan.'

'That sounds rather serious, Larry,' Louise said with a worried look.

'Yes, the doctor said that was the principal cause of my present depressive state of mind.'

'Has he prescribed any medication?'

'Yes, he's put me on a course of Prozac for a month. I've got to see him again in four weeks.'

'Prozac, yes, I've heard all about that anti-depressant drug from one of my colleagues. You can become addicted to it and must be careful not to take any other drugs while you're taking it.'

'Yes, the doctor gave me the chapter and verse on it. I started taking it this morning and I can't say that I feel any different.'

'Give it time, Larry,' Louise replied, getting up from the table, 'and just relax while you are on sick leave. When you're feeling better you could take a short break in Brighton, Hastings or Eastbourne. I want you fully fit for the wedding.'

'Don't worry, I'll be there. I'm looking forward to giving you away,' Larry said with a laugh.

'I'll see you this evening then. Remember, don't do anything to cause you stress.'

* * * * *

Immediately after Louise left the flat, Larry finished dressing and went to his car. He drove directly to Bottrell's block and parked around the corner from the building. There were few people about, but he took great care not to be seen as he quickly, but quietly climbed the stairs to Bottrell's flat. He pulled on a pair of surgical gloves and rapped on the door. Much to his surprise Bottrell opened the door almost immediately. He was wearing a silk dressing gown but nothing underneath.

'What do you want now?' Bottrell slurred, breathing whisky fumes in Howard's face.

'I just want a few words with you in private, Gary, and judging by how quickly you answered the door, you must be on your own this morning.' Howard pushed Bottrell back into the passage and pulled the door closed behind him.

'I've got nothing to say to you, so piss off and leave me alone!'

'This won't take long, Gary,' Howard said as he gave him a chopping blow across his windpipe. Bottrell fell to the floor. Howard grabbed his right arm and dragged him onto the settee. Bottrell came around coughing and choking. He tried to speak, but Howard caught him around the throat and squeezed.

'Don't try to speak, it'll hurt if you do. Now I want you to stand up and show me where you are holding those two tapes, your disguise outfit and your revolver and ammo.'

Bottrell struggled, but couldn't free himself from Howard's iron grip. He lurched forward to his bedroom. Howard followed him without taking his hands off his throat. Bottrell pointed to a wardrobe. Howard gave him a karate chop to the back of his neck and pushed him onto the bed.

Howard opened the wardrobe, looked in the top shelf and found a black plastic bag containing Bottrell's raincoat, cap, false beard and spectacles. A search of his socks and underclothing drawers revealed the two tapes, the revolver and six rounds of ammunition. He broke the revolver and removed its four unspent bullets.

As soon as Bottrell came to, Howard pointed the revolver at him and ordered him into the sitting room. He followed him with the sack.

'Now sit down, Gary, and listen to me. Our vendetta against cowboy builders is over and there is no reason whatsoever that you and I should ever meet again. So stay out of my life and I'll not have anything to do with you again.'

'You've forgotten something, Larry. I still have a

trump card—your sister. You wouldn't want her to find out what you've been doing these last weeks, would you?'

'No, I wouldn't, and if you ever tried to speak to her, I'd kill you for sure. And I'd use this gun to do it.' With that Howard placed the revolver on the sofa table.

Bottrell couldn't believe his luck. He leapt forward, snatched the gun from the table and pointed it at Howard's chest.

'You're prepared to kill me then, Gary?' Howard said in a matter-of-fact tone.

'You betcha your life, Larry—you're going soft and you're the sort of man who might even decide to confess to what you've done to the police! So I have to protect my own interests.' He squeezed the trigger, once, then again. There were two distinct clicks as the hammer fell on empty chambers. Bottrell's menacing look changed to bewilderment. He squeezed the trigger again, to hear another click.

Howard laughed. 'You've got an empty gun,' he said as Gary squeezed the trigger again. Howard reached over the table, grabbed Bottrell's wrist and banged it down on the table, knocking a half full bottle of whisky onto the floor. Bottrell screamed with pain and dropped the revolver on the floor. Howard quickly scooped it up and stuffed it under his belt. Bottrell stood up but Howard was on his feet first, put a headlock on him and pushed him face down on the floor. Kneeling on Bottrell's back, he pulled his dressing gown cord from his gown and used it to tie his wrists to his ankles. Bottrell struggled violently to release himself and cursed Howard.

Howard took a bullet from the plastic sack and inserted it in the revolver. 'Now this is my final deal, Gary. If you swear that you'll never try to contact me or my sister, I'll set you free and leave you to get back to drinking whisky. I shall take this gun, the two tapes and all your disguise items and dispose of them, along with my own disguise clothing. Of course, if you can't give me that assurance, I shall have no other option but to kill you. So, what do you say to that, Gary?'

'Of course, I'll agree to that! What else did you expect me to say?'

'It's not always what a person says, but how he says it that counts!'

'Okay, I swear over my daughter's grave, that I'll never try to make contact with you or your sister. Does that sound all right?'

'Yes, I'm sure that's the best assurance I'll get from you,' said Howard, undoing the dressing gown cord.

As soon as Bottrell was free, he leapt at Howard, knocking him over the table and striking him in the face with his fist. Howard slid sideways on the table and grabbed Bottrell around his neck. Bottrell kicked Howard's feet from under him and dived at him. Howard ducked low and Bottrell went over him, crashing on to an ornate fender that surrounded the hearth. Bottrell's forehead struck the sharp corner of the fender. His forehead was split open to the bone. Blood spurted from the wound and he remained motionless. Howard checked his pulse. There was none—Bottrell was dead.

Picking up the whisky bottle in his gloved hand, Howard emptied what was left in the bottle onto the front of Bottrell's dressing gown. He removed the bullet from the revolver and put it and the revolver into the sack. He checked all the rooms to make sure that there was no trace of him having been in the flat. He quietly opened the front door, crept down the stairs and walked to his car. He placed the plastic sack in the boot and drove off. Driving along the side of the River Thames he stopped in a secluded spot away from any buildings. He took out the two sacks, removed the revolver and bullets from Bottrell's sack and threw them into the river in different directions. He didn't want them found together. He put Bottrell's bag inside his and found a couple of half bricks on the bank of the river. He placed them in the sack, tied the top of sack and hurled it as far as he could into the river. The sack sank out of sight in seconds.

Back at his flat, he showered, changed into his house clothes and put on a dressing gown. He poured a drink, and thought over what had occurred at Bottrell's flat. It hadn't turned out as he had expected, but Bottrell being killed accidentally, the way he was, couldn't have worked out better. Now all he needed to do was to ensure that Louise never found out about his murderous vendetta against cowboy builders.

CHAPTER THIRTY ONE

Rita Petchnik let herself into Bottrell's flat. Bottrell had given her the key to save him being disturbed when she called while he was sleeping after his nightshift at the club. As she walked into the hallway, she called out: 'I'm here, Gary, make some room in the bed for me!'

She entered the sitting room and was about to cross it to enter the bedroom when she saw Bottrell's inert body, with his head lying in the hearth. She knelt down beside him, saw his blood-covered face and let out a scream. She felt for his pulse, shook his shoulder. He didn't respond. It dawned on her—Gary was dead. Seeing the empty whisky bottle, she mouthed: 'I told you, Gary, that the way you put whisky away would be the death of you.'

What she needed was a drink to steady her nerves before she rang the emergency services. She found an unopened bottle of whisky in the sideboard, opened it and poured a large measure into a tumbler and took a deep swig, which made her cough and splutter. Whisky had never been her tipple; she favoured sparkling wines, particularly champagne.

She picked up the landline telephone and dialled 999.

'What service do you require?' a calm and authoritative voice asked.

'Um… I 'm not sure, but I've just found my boyfriend dead in his flat,' Rita answered in a quavering voice.

'Stay calm and I'll transfer your call to the police and ambulance services.'

'Please let me have your name and address,' another voice asked.

'I'm Rita Petchnik and I'm phoning from my boyfriend's flat. The address is Flat 12, Bartram Court, Deptford.'

'What is your boyfriend's name?'

'Gary Bottrell.'

'Rita, please stay where you are. Police officers and paramedics will be with you in a few minutes.'

Rita took another deep swig of her whisky and sat with her back to Bottrell's body.

Ten minutes passed and there was a loud bang on the front door. Rita opened it and two paramedics, followed by a man and a woman in plain clothes waving warrant cards, entered. Rita led them into the sitting room and the paramedics immediately knelt down beside Bottrell and checked his life signs. They rose, shaking their heads. 'I'm afraid there's nothing we can do for him,' one of them said.

The male detective, who Rita thought she recognised, said, 'I'm DS Madden. You probably remember me from a previous visit. My colleague is DC Terri Burnside.'

'Yes, I do,' answered Rita in a quavering tone.

'How long have you been here?'

'About half an hour, I suppose. I never looked at my watch.'

'Have you touched, or moved anything since you came?'

'No, but I was so upset at finding him like this, I had a drink;' Rita said, pointing to her glass.

Madden looked around the room and his eyes lit on a small bookcase under the window. He looked over the books, removed one and read its title on its spine. 'Now that's very interesting,' he mused. He turned to DC Burnside and said, 'Terri, I have something I must do straightaway. Phone in for the Duty DI, the Forensic Team, and the Coroner's Officer. Tell the Duty DI, I think it's Rutledge, that I've dashed off to follow up a lead which might help us clear up the cowboy builder case.'

Turning to Rita, Madden said, 'You'll have to stay here with Terri, until the detective inspector has seen you.'

Madden went to his car and drove to Howard's flat. He rang the doorbell; the door was opened by Howard, who looked questioningly at Madden.

'Good morning Mr Howard,' said Madden, passing his warrant card in front of Howard's face. 'I'm Detective Sergeant Madden.'

'Oh, yes, I remember you. Congratulations on your promotion to detective sergeant. You must be satisfying your superiors that you are doing something right to deserve a promotion,' Howard said in a jocular tone.

'That's what I want to talk to you about, Mr Howard. May I come in?'

'Of course you may. Being on sick leave is not all it's cracked up to be. It can get quite boring, so having someone to chat with helps to pass the day.'

Madden made no reply and followed Howard into the sitting room.

'Can I offer you a cup of tea, coffee or a cold drink, Sergeant?'

'No thank you, but I'd like to ask you a few questions. Before I start, I tried to contact you at your office, but your manager told me you were on sick leave. Nothing serious, I hope?'

'I'm under my doctor, who has diagnosed my condition and has told me that I am suffering from post-traumatic stress disorder, attributable to my experiences in Iraq and Afghanistan.'

'Oh, I wasn't aware of that, Mr Howard.'

'Now, please sit down and fire away with your questions, Sergeant.'

'Before the questioning, I have some sad news for you.'

'Oh yes, and what's that all about?'

'Gary Bottrell has been found dead in his flat at Deptford.'

'Oh, has he? But why should I find that news to be sad when I don't even know the man?'

'Come; come now, Mr Howard, you know who I'm talking about. He is an ex-soldier as you are and a partner of yours in the murder of seven so-called cowboy builders.'

'I don't know him and I've never heard of him.'

'He was a corporal in the military police.'

'Now, I seem to have heard these questions before and my answers are the same as I gave before. Thankfully, during my twenty-two years' service in the army, I didn't have much to do with the military police and I certainly never knew one named Gary Bottrell!'

Madden made direct eye contact with Howard before he spoke. 'Well, here's a new question for you. Where were you on Monday night at about 8.45?'

Howard gave a short laugh. 'That's an easy question. I was sitting in this very chair watching a film on television.'

'Was anyone else present who could corroborate that?'

'No, my sister was out with her boyfriend at a theatre.'

'What was the title of the film you were watching?'

'It was called *Harry Brown*. It was its first showing on television and being a fan of Michael Caine, I particularly wanted to see it.'

'Yes, I saw it at the cinema when it first came out, Larry. You don't mind me calling you by your first name, do you?'

'No, feel free to use it. The way things are going I can see us becoming close friends.'

'What did you think about the way the film ended?'

'I'm sure that most of its audiences appreciated that Harry Brown had justifiably rid his neighbourhood of some very nasty characters and deserved to get away with what he'd done. But of course it was completely out of character with the way things happen in real life. Crime must not pay and justice must prevail.'

'Ah, so you are quite prepared to pay for the crimes that you have committed, Larry!'

Howard shook his head from side to side. 'Now that's enough, Detective Sergeant Madden, you're beginning to bore me with all your ridiculous accusations. I shall have to ask you to leave. If you think I've committed a crime then arrest me or leave me alone. You seem to be forgetting that I am on sick leave suffering from post-traumatic stress disorder and the stress you are causing me is worsening my condition.'

Madden gave a sympathetic look. 'I'm sorry that my questioning has been so stressful for you, Larry, I'm just trying to get to the truth. I've just one more question to ask you, then I'll go.'

Howard sighed deeply and his eyebrows rose. 'Okay, let's hear it!'

'Have you ever read a book entitled *Strangers on a Train?* It was written by Patricia Highsmith, or have you seen the film, based on the novel, which was made by Alfred Hitchcock in 1951?'

Howard shook his head and looked perplexed. 'No, I can't say that I have. What are you on about now, Sergeant? Is this to be some sort of quiz you're giving me?'

'No, the question I have asked has great relevance to the case I am investigating. As you say you've not read the novel, nor seen the film, I'd better give you a brief idea of the plot. Two young men meet on a train and talk about the two people in their lives who are causing them to wish that they were dead. The psychotic one, let's call him Bottrell, suggests that they swop murders. This, he says, will then enable them to establish cast iron alibis for the times of the murders—'

'Stop right there Madden, I can see where you're taking this, but it's sheer bunkum. You'd better leave now, or I'll call your superiors.'

'All right, Mr Howard, I'll leave you with this to think about—I found a copy of *Strangers on a Train* in Bottrell's bookcase! Next time I interview you it'll be at the police station and you'll be under arrest!' Madden blurted out as he rose and left the room.

Howard heard the front door slam as Madden left the flat. He went to his sideboard, took out a bottle of brandy and a glass and poured a double measure. As he sipped his drink, he thought about what next he needed to do with some urgency.

CHAPTER THIRTY TWO

'What are you planning to do today, Larry?' Louise said as they sat down for breakfast.

'I haven't made up my mind yet, but I do feel like a run-out somewhere.'

'Yes, that's what you should do. Why don't you have a drive down to the coast—Hastings, Brighton, Eastbourne, or somewhere like that and spend a couple of days in a bed and breakfast cottage? The weather forecast promises that it will be dry and sunny on the coast for the next few days.'

'I might just do that, Louise. It's been years since I was down there. Remember, we had some great times in the past when I came home on leave and we took mum and dad down there. They loved it. They always said that it was better than any foreign holiday.'

'Yes, I miss them too, Larry.'

'That's it then, as soon as you leave for school, I'll get myself ready. I think I'll make for Eastbourne and stay there for two or three days. I'll keep in touch to let you know when I'll be returning.'

'I'm sure you'll benefit by having a few days in the sunshine and fresh air and no worries about work.'

The letter flap made a noise and they heard a plopping sound as the mail—most likely of the junk variety—dropping on the hall carpet.

'The post's early this morning,' said Larry as he left the table to collect it. He returned with the mail. 'The usual junk, your Teachers' NUT magazine and some catalogues. But there's a letter from the insurance company.' He hastily slit open the envelope with his table knife. His face beamed with delight as he read the letter and waved the enclosed cheque. 'They've settled our claim in full.' He passed the letter and cheque to Louise. 'Pay this into your account when you go out for lunch today.'

'This should be yours, Larry. You paid the deposit for mum and dad's house and helped them with their mortgage repayments.'

'No, the money is yours, Louise. Call it a wedding present. There's enough to buy a small house or put down a big deposit on a larger one.'

'Thanks a million, Larry! I can't wait to tell Tony. I'm sure he'll be as thrilled as I am. We can start looking for a suitable property right away.'

'It's made my day as well. I'm so very pleased that you and Tony won't have any problems in scrimping and saving to buy a house.'

'Yes, it's truly a wonderful wedding present, Larry. Speaking of the wedding, don't forget you have a new suit to order. Perhaps you could call into a good tailor to get measured before you leave for Eastbourne.'

'Yes, don't worry, I'll see to that. Now, you'd better

get your skates on or you'll be late for school. I'll clear up the breakfast things after you've gone. I shan't be here when you get back this evening, but I'll keep in touch with my mobile.'

Louise put on her top coat, grabbed her briefcase and went to the front door. Larry followed to say goodbye. She dropped her briefcase, flung her arms around his neck and kissed him on the cheek. Releasing him she looked up at him, a look of adoration in her eyes 'You're the best brother anyone could have! Enjoy your stay in Eastbourne and I'll see you in a few days' time.'

Larry gave her a hug, kissed her and said: 'Goodbye, Louise.'

Larry cleared the breakfast dishes, washed up and ran the vacuum around the sitting room before he made ready to leave. Next, he packed a suitcase with a grey lounge suit, his REME tie, for eveningwear, six shirts, three sets of underwear, socks, sandals, hiking boots, a gabardine windcheater jacket, a pair of jeans and a baseball cap.

Before he left he checked his car's oil and water, and tyre pressures.

He stopped at his local off licence and bought a bottle of Remy Martin, a tin of fruit drops and a bottle of water.

The distance he had to travel to Eastbourne was about seventy miles, but he was in no hurry and kept at a steady speed of about fifty miles per hour.

Arriving in Eastbourne, he went to his favourite restaurant and had a lunch of lamb chops, new potatoes and peas, followed by two scoops of vanilla ice cream—

his favourite meal. Afterwards he relaxed at his table for about fifteen minutes with a newspaper and two cups of coffee. He left the restaurant a little past one o'clock and went to the Strand Hotel, one of Eastbourne's upmarket hotels. He registered and presented his credit card to the receptionist, who told him that his room would be available for occupancy at two o'clock. For something to do while he was waiting to get into his room, he went to the hotel's hairdressing salon and had a haircut and a manicure. He went back to the reception desk at two o'clock and collected his room key. He collected his suitcase from his car in the hotel garage and went to his room. He unpacked his suitcase and put his clothes in the wardrobe and chest of drawers.

He left the hotel at two-thirty. The sun was still high in the sky and the weather was unseasonably warm. It became very warm in the car, which was not air-conditioned, so he took off his jacket and placed it on the front passenger seat. He drove west from Eastbourne along the road leading to Seaford and turned off the road a few miles before reaching East Dean and, driving along rough tracks, headed for Beachy Head. He stopped about ten yards from the cliff edge and admired the view of the coastline in the west and the east through his car windows. He opened the brandy bottle and poured a generous measure into a thermos flask lid. He sipped his drink while he marvelled at the unrivalled beauty of the coastline. He sat there for about half an hour drinking brandy and thinking of the times he had visited the site with his parents and Louise.

He decided that he would get a better view of the coastline and the ships passing through the English Channel if he got out of his car and used his binoculars. He collected his binoculars from the boot, and, ignoring the signs warning people not to go too close to the edge of the cliff, he walked to about five feet from the cliff's edge. As he had believed it would be, the view from that spot was even more revealing and he stood there for several minutes scanning the coastline and the passing ships.

Mr and Mrs Tom Barker were walking their Labrador along the cliff, about fifty yards from the edge. 'Tom, look at that man down there. He's taking a risk being so close the cliff's edge, especially since we've recently had the cliff breaking away at that point.'

Tom turned and looked to where his wife was pointing. 'He seems to know what he's doing, Doris. He must be getting an amazing view with his binoculars.'

Howard heard their voices and turned to see who was there. They gave him a friendly wave. He waved back and in doing so, dropped his binoculars. Bending down to pick them up, he lost his balance, fell backwards and rolled over the cliff's edge to fall the 530 feet to the rock-strewn shoreline below.

'Oh my God!' screamed Doris. 'That poor man's gone over the edge!'

'Yes, I saw him go, Doris, and I don't expect he could have survived such a fall,' Tom said, taking his mobile phone from his jacket pocket. 'We'd better ring the emergency services.'

* * * * *

Tom and Doris Barker remained on the cliff top until the police arrived. A sergeant and two constables got out of their car and joined them.

'You phoned the station and told the control room operator what you saw, Mr Barker?'

'Yes, Sergeant, I told him everything that happened.'

Doris, who was distraught and almost in tears, added, 'Yes, it was a shocking accident; I just hope that us waving to him didn't cause him to fall.'

'No, you shouldn't blame yourselves,' the sergeant said consolingly. 'The man was taking a great risk, standing where he was. It's not the first time someone's gone over the edge here and I don't suppose this one will be the last.'

'Sarge,' the constable said, 'I've had a message from the duty inspector. He says that an RAF helicopter is on its way. When they arrive a crewman will be winched down to try and recover the body.'

'That's good; I don't know how else we could recover the body. Pete, you stay on the spot to guide the helicopter over where the man fell.'

Turning to the other officer, the sergeant said, 'Mike, see if you can find anything in the car to identify him.'

Mike returned with Howard's jacket and handed it to the sergeant. The sergeant went through the pockets and withdrew the Strand Hotel room key, Howard's wallet and a receipt for a deposit paid for a suit, which was to be made by an expensive south London tailor.

'We're in luck here, Mike, we know where he's staying and we have his home address on his driving licence. Radio the information to the duty inspector who will be able arrange for the man's next-of-kin to be informed and for his personal effects to be collected from the hotel. I wish all the cliff accidents were as easy as this one to deal with.'

'You're certainly right about that, Sarge,' replied Mike.

The End

ND - #0485 - 270225 - C0 - 203/127/18 - PB - 9781909304680 - Matt Lamination